Icebound Attraction

Our books are also available in e-book.

Find our catalog on:
https://cherry-publishing.com/en/

NINA NORRIS

Icebound Attraction

© Nina Norris, 2024

© Cherry Publishing, 2024

ISBN: 978-1-80116-806-9

1

Emily

"Shit!" I exclaim when I see the message on my phone. "Mom! Mom! They've just canceled my flight!"

My heart races as I frantically scan the United airline app to figure out what's going on.

With my flight leaving in four hours, I was ready to hit the road for the airport.

My mother's voice echoes in the hallway, coupled with rapid footsteps in my direction.

"It says something about problems on scheduled flights."

"Shit," sighs my mother in turn.

She grabs her laptop and tries, like me, to figure out what we should do next. But the Internet isn't cooperative, and my app's chatbot only tells me to talk to the airport staff.

"The only solution is to go," announces Mom, shrugging her shoulders.

"You're probably right."

I close my slightly overstuffed suitcase, grab my hand luggage and my bag. I place it by the door to put on my jacket and shoes.

My father comes running to say goodbye. He's been sulking for days because his baby is leaving the nest to go to university. Honestly, I can't help but smile at his scowl. Even so, he pulls me into his big arms and holds me unusually close.

"Dad! Dad! I'm having trouble breathing," I say in a choked voice.

Reluctantly, he lets go and starts carrying my luggage to the car.

I was right to say goodbye to my sisters this afternoon. Goodbyes are definitely not my thing, and it saves us any more tears in the rush of the situation.

I follow my father to the car, where my mother is already waiting. He looks at me sadly - as he often does these days - and I place a big kiss on his cheek.

"I love you, Dad."

He just grunts the same thing and shuffles back to the veranda, where he stops and looks at us longingly. My mother is already sitting in the driver's seat and starts the car. I climb in and look out of the window. I take one last look at our house, and a mixture of fear, excitement and anticipation settles over me. Texas has always been my home and I love it here, but it's time to start a new chapter in my life.

I wave to my father, and as we drive off, all previous feelings are replaced by overwhelming curiosity. I'm finally going to study journalism at university - and in the Big Apple! I wonder if it'll be like the movies.

Sex, booze and parties...

I shake my head. I'd rather not think about it. Sure, I've got nothing against partying or getting drunk, but it's absolutely not my objective. I want to concentrate on my studies and get good grades, not hang around like an alcoholic corpse in the bed of a guy whose first name I won't remember.

I imagine walking across campus and being greeted by my classmates. How I'll work diligently in class and fall into bed at night, satisfied. Inevitably, the corners of my mouth turn up.

I can't wait!

When we finally arrive at the airport, a message appears on my cell phone informing me that I've been transferred to a flight for tomorrow afternoon - with a two-hour layover in Washington.

Great.

We make our way to the counter. On the notice board, several canceled flights are flashing. So, I'm not the only one. Before I can even open my mouth, my mother takes the lead. I think I'll always be her little girl... Patiently, I stand back and let her do her thing.

"My daughter's flight today has been canceled. She has another one tomorrow afternoon. Is there a hotel room for her in this case? Does the airline pay for it or not?" she asks the counter clerk, slightly stressed.

"Yes, ma'am. Everything is taken care of. Your daughter can go to this hotel."

The young woman from the airline hands us a document stating that the night is offered to me in an establishment not far from the airport, and all the other details are noted on it.

I turn to my mother, whose eyes shine with a suspicious moisture. From now on, she has to leave me, and I must go on alone. We hug each other and both fight back tears.

"Take care of yourself, darling," she murmurs, hastily wiping her face. "Let us know how it goes. And send us a message when you're on the plane! Don't be careless!"

I nod, smiling as much as I can, swallowing the big lump in my throat. I take my bag from her and head for the buses to the hotel, pulling my suitcase behind me. If I turn around one more time, I'm going to start crying, that's for sure.

Once there, I have to wait a while at the reception. Many passengers who couldn't catch the plane today are spending the night there, like me. I smirk. So many people with so many different stories. Sometimes I wish I could interview them all and write about them, because I'm sure everyone has a story to tell that's worth sharing. Journalism is a real passion for me, and I often embark on dreams like that.

Once in my room, I take out my cell phone to send a text message to my best friend.

Maddie's been at NYU for a year and she's so excited for me to finally join her, she's been sending me a countdown every morning for weeks. I'm sure she'll be disappointed that I'm not arriving until later.

I tell her about my latest adventures and a few seconds later, she's already answering me.

* Sweetie, I can hardly believe you're finally on your way! I'm so happy! WTF is this delay? Once you're here, I'll take care of you like a mother bird takes care of her chick.

A laugh escapes me. Maddie has always been good at bringing a smile to my lips. I've known her for what seems like forever, and we were in high school together. I can't wait to see her!

The next day, when I'm finally seated on the plane, a smile of satisfaction stretches across my face. I'm almost there... In a few hours, I'll finally be there!

The flight goes off without a hitch. Once I've landed, I don't have to wait long for my suitcase. I hoist it off the conveyor belt and hurry towards the exit. No sooner have I passed through the automatic doors than I already see her - Maddie, beaming. She's holding a huge sign with my name written on it in a multitude of sequins. Usually, such attention makes me uncomfortable, but this time I don't care. I just want to hug my best friend. I run to her and hug her so tightly that we both nearly fall over.

"You've been waiting a long time, gorgeous! I'm so glad you're finally here!" she laughs, giving me a big kiss on the cheek.

"What a trip!" I mumble, as we walk arm in arm towards the exit.

All the way to the dorm we chat and laugh. It's so good to be near her again. Together, we're simply better - like honey tea. We have a saying: 'perfect separately, unbeatable together'.

Finally, we park and cross the campus. I'm already feeling nauseous, so apprehensive. I'm really here! At New York City University! I look around me in awe.

Can someone pinch me so I know it's real?

Maddie pinches my hip and I squeal.

"What the hell are you doing?"

She giggles, as if she's read my mind.

"You're staring so hard, I thought I'd bring you back to the moment like this!"

I can't stop laughing. It's always been that way. In a frightening way, Maddie's thoughts and mine seem to be linked.

We keep walking and pass a magnificent tree that looks almost magical in the light of the streetlamps. Then we find ourselves in front of the residence. It's not the most modern building in the world, but it's something. After all, the facade can be deceiving.

Maddie has her own room, while I could only afford a shared one. And it was impossible for both of us to take one for administrative reasons.

I really hope I'm going to get on well with my roommate...

We head for the entrance and Maddie helps me with my luggage. My new room is on the second floor. Thank God there's an elevator and it looks pretty modern. It would have been impossible to climb even two more stairs with this heavy suitcase.

The elevator opens with a *pling* and I look directly for my room number, '220'. It's obviously at the end of the corridor.

My heart races as I knock on the door. I wonder what's waiting for me behind the door, or rather, *who's* waiting for me behind the door?

"Come in!" resounds a voice a little too high-pitched.

Maddie and I look at each other briefly before I open the door.

I'm speechless as I enter the room. It's tastefully decorated. In the center is a small wooden table with two chairs, and to the left and right are the sleeping areas. In one corner, there's a comfortable-looking miniature sofa and a small TV; while in the other is a small kitchenette. At the window, a graceful brunette skillfully arranges a curtain.

"Hi! I'm Emily, your new roommate," I say with a smile.

The interested party turns mischievously and looks me up and down.

"We need to change your taste in shoes," she declares.

"It's... I..." I stammer, taken aback.

My roommate then starts laughing, approaches me and gives me a warm hug.

"Gotcha! I'm Cassy, nice to meet you!"

She lets go of me and looks questioningly at Maddie.

"Uh, this is Maddie, my best friend, she studies here too."

Maddie also gets a hug.

Phew, I'm lucky! I immediately feel at ease in Cassy's presence. She has a pleasant charisma, a warm gaze and obviously a sharp sense of humor.

"Come in, come in, sit down! Can I offer you something to drink? Some coffee? Some tea? How was your trip? Where are you from?"

Well, she talks a little too much. I'll have to get used to it.

We chat briefly and exchange the usual information. She's originally from California, is studying fashion - which doesn't seem surprising given her pronounced taste for decoration - and is also new here at the university. Then she shows me to my personal space. It's small, but also beautifully decorated.

Maddie helps me unpack.

"How about a welcome drink downstairs at the café?" says my best friend, wagging her eyebrows.

I'm completely exhausted, but at the same time too excited to go to sleep right away, so I nod. We ask Cassy if she'd like to come with us.

"Only if you wear other shoes," she shouts from her bed.

The three of us laugh and I grab a pair of booties.

"What do you think of these?"

Cassy's gaze shifts from the boots to me and back again. After a moment's reflection, she finally says:

"Acceptable."

"I'm glad," I giggle, and we set off laughing.

I don't know what I expected from a campus café, but it was clearly not *this*. It's reminiscent of a 1920s speakeasy[1] . The decor, the atmosphere, the music - it's all there! I immediately feel at ease. It's not very crowded, probably because it's a weeknight.

No sooner are we seated at a table than a waitress is waving frantically at us. She has short blond hair, a few piercings on her face and tattooed arms.

"Maddie, what a surprise!"

My best friend greets her with a smile.

"This is Ella! Ella, this is my best friend Emily, fresh from Texas, and her roommate Cassy."

"Delighted! The first round of welcome drinks is on the

---

[1] A speakeasy serving alcoholic beverages during the Prohibition era in the United States, from around 1920 to 1930.

house," says Ella. "What will it be?"

Maddie orders two freshly squeezed juices and gives Cassy a quizzical look.

She looks at us conspiratorially.

"Tonight, I'm going wild! Green tea, please."

The three of us giggle and the waitress returns to the counter.

I let my gaze wander around the café and stop at a group of boys. They look rather sporty and, from the way they behave with each other, they seem more like a herd of teenagers than students.

Maybe the soccer team?

Let's hope not! I know I'm going to have to interview one of them as part of my journalism course - and also because I'm joining the university newspaper - and they don't make me want to approach them at all!

That's when a guy - admittedly hot - notices my stare and gives me an air kiss. I wrinkle my nose and look away, blushing.

Why can't they behave like normal people?

"Don't let the jocks throw you off. Most of them are looking for flings and are trying to seduce all the new girls," says Maddie.

Cassy also nods, irritated.

"But whatever, today we're celebrating the fact that you're finally here! To hell with everything else!"

Then the waitress returns with our drinks and we toast.

"Here's to an exciting year," says Cassy solemnly.

The tingle in my belly is full of promise as I take my first sip with a smile. I can't wait to find out what's in store for me.

★★★

On my first official day, I'm up early. The excitement of

meeting the student newspaper team and my long to-do list drag me out of bed at 6:30.

I put on my bathrobe and set off in search of coffee. A pleasant smell of breakfast is already wafting up my nose. Cassy is sitting at the little table in the center of our room, enjoying waffles.

"Good morning, sunshine! Are you an early riser too?" she exclaims cheerfully.

"Hello, Cassy. I'm trying, yes, but what I really need now is a…"

Before I can finish my sentence, she gets up and heads for the coffee machine, explaining how to use it and showing me where to find everything I need.

With my steaming mug in hand, we sit down together.

"Before you go to the paper, maybe you should take a shower and fix your hair," Cassy says, looking at me intently.

"Oh, thank you, good idea! I was actually thinking of going out there in a bathrobe," I reply sarcastically.

She giggles, stands up and puts on her jacket.

"Well, it's a good thing I suggested it, then! I'll see you later, I've got to go!"

She gives me a little wave before closing the door behind her. I savor the rest of my coffee and, above all, the calm. This early in the morning, conversations are very difficult for me!

Maddie said she'd pick me up at 7:30, so I'd better jump in the shower. I didn't really look at the bathroom yesterday. It's small, but functional. Simple and modern. Obviously, Cassy hasn't decorated the place yet! But I'm sure it won't be long before she does.

As I apply my mascara, there's already a knock on the door. *Is Maddie on time? That would be a first!*

I greet her with enthusiasm. I still can't believe my best friend is finally with me. I really missed her.

"Are you ready?" she asks.

"Don't we have time for a coffee?" I retort, horrified.

"Only if you want to be late on the first day!"

She points to the empty cup on the table and smiles.

"And you've already had one. I thought you wanted to work on your caffeine addiction," she remarks.

When she sees my pout, she gives in.

"OK! We can pick one up on the way."

"Hallelujah!" I shout with satisfaction, and we're off.

It's a twenty-minute walk to the student newspaper offices. I take advantage of this breath of fresh air to analyze the hustle and bustle around us and observe the campus. It's still surreal for me to finally be here.

We enter a modern building where all my journalism courses will be held and where the newspaper offices are also located. It's imposing and also a little intimidating.

Once there, Maddie, who's also part of the editorial team, introduces me to everyone, including the editor-in-chief, David, whom I had already spoken to on the phone, and she shows me to my office. Everyone has their own little corner, and there's a conference room for meetings. The computer equipment is state-of-the-art, and there seems to be no shortage of anything.

"You'll be working for the newspaper's sports section. Your first assignment will be to interview the captain of the ice hockey team. He can be a bit... special. But don't worry, you'll do just fine," Maddie explains.

I frown, puzzled. I didn't even know the university had an ice hockey team, and I know nothing about the sport. In high school, I specialized in basketball. And the captain is... *special?* Is that why they're sending me to the front? Because no one else will talk to him? Maybe it's some kind of test or hazing. I see it as a way of proving my worth to them. Whatever, I'll get through it! I'm new here and I'm going to prove myself. In my head, I'm already going over the information I need to get to write a good article. The deadline is Wednesday. So, I've got five days to learn everything I can about the sport and, above all, convince the team captain to grant me an interview. Maddie said he knows I will come, but not that he agrees to a Q&A...

Back to work!

2

Liam

We've just finished training and I'm sitting - still all sweaty - in front of Coach Franklyn's office. He's asked me to wait for him here, and since he's the coach, well, I comply without question. He probably wants to talk to me about next week's game and go over strategy.

"You were good today," he says as he enters the room.

"Thanks, Coach. The team was also in great shape. I think we can easily win the next game, especially if we base it on..."

"That's good to hear, but that's not why you're here," he cuts me off. "I've managed to get the university's administration to agree that this year's student newspaper will feature more ice hockey. It'll attract spectators and sponsors. Maybe a sports agent will hear about you too. It wouldn't hurt."

When I hear the words 'sports agent', my eyes light up. My ultimate dream is to become a professional player. I'd do anything to get an agent to come and see us and show him what I'm capable of - and what the team is capable of. Regular articles in the student newspaper might actually help. Although... most journalists on campus are looking for scandal, or already have a story in mind that they want confirmed with targeted questions. It annoys me to no end. It's true that I've never been very gentle with them. That's probably why our games are hardly ever covered by the student newspaper. Most of the time, we just get an insert with the results. But with more detailed articles, we could attract more attention, and also recruit new players. We need new blood."

I nod and let the coach continue.

"One of the journalists will be at Monday's game and will ask you a few questions afterwards. Will that be all right?"

I nod, docile.

"No problem, coach. It's right up my alley."

"Please behave yourself, Liam... It's important that we're presented in a favorable light. And don't forget that with the start of the season, parties and girl drama will need to be kept to a minimum. Do you think you can avoid flirting with half the university for a while?"

I laugh out loud.

"Don't worry, coach, I'll show my best side!"

I give him my most enticing smile, but it has no impact on him. Coach Franklyn looks at me seriously.

"That's exactly what worries me, Liam."

I raise both hands and look innocent, but the coach remains unperturbed.

"All right, all right. I'll behave, I promise."

As I leave the room and the door closes behind me, I hear a sigh and can't help but smile.

An interview with a snobbish journalist... Hm, it might turn out to be a lot of fun after all...

I spend the rest of the evening with my friends. We've organized a barbecue and are drinking beers while discussing hockey.

I should be studying for my exams, but before a game, I prefer to let off steam with my mates. Ice hockey is my life.

Icebound Attraction

Who needs a degree in business management, right? On my skates, I'm in my element. I forget all my worries and just concentrate on the game.

Sometimes I imagine my father in the audience, proudly exulting as I slam puck after puck into the opposing goal. But the bastard took off when I was only 4. He left his wife and three kids for his secretary. What a piece of shit...

I put the thought out of my mind, down my beer and set off in search of a pleasant distraction. Sitting in a corner, a beautiful redhead smiles at me.

That's exactly what I need!

I approach her. We chat for a while and she seems attracted to me. That's not unusual. Women fall for the team captain, it's inherent in the role. That and my good looks always hit the jackpot.

When I ask her if she'd like to see my room, with as much finesse as if I'd asked her directly if she'd sleep with me, she nods excitedly. Sometimes it's so simple it's boring. But tonight, I don't want to sleep alone.

★★★

The final whistle sounds and the whole stadium erupts in joy. What a game! We've just won our first of the season, and I couldn't be prouder. Let's keep it up, and we'll have a great place in the qualifiers.

I'm on the ice with my teammates and we're hugging and screaming. The intensive training has definitely paid off.

Suddenly, I notice a pretty blonde standing at the edge of the stands, notepad and pen in hand.

What's she doing here? And why is she looking at us like she's waiting for something?

That's when it all clicks: someone from the student newspaper is coming to interview me today, that's right! I was expecting an annoying guy with thick glasses, not such an attractive girl... Immediately, any preconceptions I might have about her work go up in smoke. Intrigued, I approach her as the spectators gradually leave the rink and my team's jubilation subsides.

Her smile is warm and welcoming as I greet her.

"Hi, I'm Emily, sports journalist for the university newspaper," she introduces herself, holding out her hand.

It's very formal. I like it. But I prefer the body attached to this hand...

"I'm Liam Scott," I reply, shaking her hand in return, which is surprisingly soft and pleasantly warm. "You've come to interview the team captain, is that right?"

I smile and tap the 'C' on my shirt. She nods.

"Yes, that's it! Your team played a great game today. I'd like to ask you a few questions, if you have the time."

Despite myself, I frown.

Does she already have an idea of the scoop she's going to drop like a bomb in her rag? Let's face it, the university newspaper is a load of crap. It's like they're trying to create a buzz to get attention. What do they expect? To uncover the campus gossip of the century and win a Pulitzer? But either way, Coach told me to make an effort, and if it'll draw attention to us, then it's good.

"I've got all the time in the world for a journalist as pretty as you," I announce.

She raises her eyes to the sky and steps back to sit on a bench. I can't help but smile as I follow her.

Oh, this is going to be fun...

As her questions progress, I realize that she has a pretty good grasp of the subject. Already, she's using the right vocabulary, which is usually pretty rare when we're asked about our performances, and she seems to have a pretty professional take on the game.

"How do you manage to reconcile top-level sport with your studies?" she asks.

I frown.

This is it. The burning question. There had to be one...

"I organize myself accordingly. Of course, training takes time, but I don't give up on my classes. It's very important," I lie.

I note that she frowns slightly, adding an extra charm to her concentrated air.

You're the one who should be concentrating, Liam!

"Yet you don't seem to be in the lecture halls very often..."

"Is it an interview for the sports paper or a report for the attendance office?" I retort, suddenly annoyed.

"Oh... I... Sorry... I didn't think my question would bother you."

She scratches her forehead feverishly, rereading her notes.

"As captain, what message would you like to pass on to your teammates and fans after this game?"

"I'm proud of their performance. If we don't give up, we can qualify. As for the fans, their unfailing support is invaluable. It's their encouragement that pushes us to surpass ourselves," I reply calmly.

She seems to notice that my tone of voice is more neutral, and scribbles a few more words before looking up at me. Two lakes, a perfect blue, where I lose myself for a moment.

"Would it be possible for us to debrief like this at the end of the next few games?" she suggests, a little embarrassed.

I'm pretty sure she doesn't have a choice. And anyway, I don't have it either.

"Are you asking me out, Emily?" I suggest, to lighten the mood, and also because I can't help myself.

Suddenly, her cheeks turn a lovely shade of red and I notice her body tense up.

"I... No... It's... er... for the paper..." she stammers.

"I was only joking," I assert, trying to throw her off balance.

"Ha... Right... Um, so?"

"Yes, we can do that. We'll meet up at the end of the games."

She nods, satisfied, her face still tinged with pink. Her blond hair sweeps across her shoulders for a moment, and I watch her in spite of myself, my eyes squinting.

Is the hunt on, Liam?

"Well, thanks Liam for taking the time."

"Thank you for your professionalism, Emily."

I give her my most charming smile and she takes her leave, smiling slightly. I watch her a moment longer, registering the movement of her body as it leaves my field of vision. Coach Franklyn's words echo in my head. It'll be far from easy not to flirt with her, but I've behaved relatively well today.

Anyway, she was attentive and seemed genuinely interested in who I was - outside of ice hockey. In a way, it felt good to talk to someone who didn't just see me as the team captain or the campus womanizer. I can't remember the last time someone really listened to me.

She also seems smart and passionate. It's a change from the girls I usually hang out with.

I shake my head.

It's my last year at university and I want to be spotted by an agent to have a better chance at the draft. It's her professionalism I can count on, not her killer ass or her charisma!

"How did the interview go?"

Coach Franklyn's voice draws me out of my thoughts.

"She fell for it, of course," I reply with a big smile.

He frowns morosely.

"Liam! This isn't funny. Can you take this seriously for once?"

I roll my eyes.

"It went well, Coach. I promised you I'd behave, and I did. She asked some interesting questions. We agreed to debrief after the next few games so she could have more material for her articles."

"Oh, it's good she's coming back! I take it you've kept your word. I'm relieved. Anyway, great game today! You're really in shape. I'm proud of you," he says, tapping me on the shoulder.

"Thanks, Coach," I reply as I head for the changing rooms, eager to get out of my uniform and into the shower.

The coach is on my tail and I can already feel what's coming next. The usual talk about responsibility, effort, blah, blah, blah...

"Guys! Great game!" he proclaims in the locker room.

The team responds by shouting from all sides. The atmosphere is festive and everyone makes a comment.

"If you keep this up, we'll be the best of the season! I know you want to party, drink and have fun. But please remember that you all have classes tomorrow. Your academic results must come first if you want to succeed in your studies. No agent is going to want you if your grades aren't up."

As he says this, he gives me a special look. The guys groan in chorus and practically beg the coach to at least come and have a beer with them.

"Well, okay..." he finally gives in, still reluctant, and loud cheers erupt.

When we arrive at the 'sports bar', showered and fresh, it's already a buzz. Thunderous applause erupts as the crowd notices us, and countless people congratulate me and tap me on the shoulder.

I take advantage of this attention to spot an attractive student watching me. Eventually, she approaches me, and her eyes reveal what she wants: me. In such cases, we might as well avoid long speeches, don't you think? Normally, I wouldn't say no, I'd just have a bit of fun and go my own way. No stress, no obligations. But tonight, I just want to party with my boys and celebrate the start of the season. Unless she offers me a one night stand in the bar's bathroom, she won't be coming home on my arm, that's for sure.

My alarm goes off and I feel like I've been run over by a truck. It's already time to go to class. Shit... Will anyone really notice if I don't go? I'm too exhausted to dig myself out anyway. Well, I'm also hungover. But we had to celebrate our success properly, didn't we! I've already skipped countless times, but one more won't go unnoticed, will it?

I turn on my side and close my eyes.

When I wake up, it's already noon and my stomach is rumbling. Unfortunately, I have nothing to eat in my dorm room. I only keep the bare minimum here and the cupboards are definitely empty. This leaves me with only the campus café to hope I can swallow something that will keep me going. With a big yawn, I swing out of bed. In no time at all, I'm ready to face the sun and the crowd of students. My headache is gone and I feel better than when my alarm went off several hours earlier.

I open my door, trying to get my hair in order. As I look up into the hallway, my heart seizes with dread: Coach Franklyn is standing in front of me, staring at me with his usual air of seriousness.

Fuck, he is going to give me a heart attack!

My shoulders immediately slump. I feel like I'm going to take the brunt of this...

"Liam. I'm glad you're awake. You weren't in class today, so I thought I'd better check on you myself."

His ironic tone does not go unnoticed.

"Sorry, Coach. I got... a little food poisoning, and... uh..."

Yeah, I'm running out of arguments. That's lame. Coach

Franklyn looks disappointed and I can't deny I deserve it.

"Damn it, Liam, we've been over this dozens of times! Less partying and more studying! If you don't have an impeccable record, you can kiss the NHL goodbye[2]! As you know, graduation isn't compulsory, but it's the only way to ensure your future. We don't know what tomorrow will bring! You're lucky enough to be able to study, so don't throw it all away..."

I sigh.

"Yeah, I know, I know. I'm sorry coach, I'll try harder, I swear."

"It's the least you can do. You're excluded from training today. Catch up on the lessons you've missed, and you'll be able to join in tomorrow."

Incredulous, I stare at him. Just as I'm about to protest, he cuts me off.

"I am adamant, Liam."

I raise my hands in resignation and nod.

Without another word, he leaves me with a guilty conscience. I exhale with difficulty and head for the campus café. I still have to eat.

As I approach the entrance, I see Emily sitting by one of the windows. She's with another student and seems to be enjoying herself, judging by the way she's laughing and tossing her long blonde hair back. It's been a long time since I've heard such a hearty, sincere laugh. She seems so carefree and happy. And it has to be said, too, that this girl is more of the self-aware hottie type. I bet she's a bit of a killjoy around the edges. It would be a good challenge to try and make her fall for you...

Damn it, Liam. Just let it go.

It's definitely a distraction I don't need. Besides, Coach Franklyn would cut my balls off if he realized what I was thinking of doing with our resident reporter!

---

[2] National Hockey League.

I shake my head and walk straight past her without looking.

Once at the counter, I greet my best friend Chase with a big smile. He's on duty today, since he's working there as an extra, and flirting - again - with a customer. Typical! He just can't help himself!

"Chase! Still trying to win over the clientele? Do you talk to them before or after the first date about your quirks in the sack?" I exclaim to display it.

He opens wide offended eyes, and his current crush takes the opportunity to go away. I burst out laughing as he grunts.

"Coffee, I presume?" he asks.

"That's right! You're very kind."

"You've had a rude wake-up call, from the look on your face."

I make a little pout, as if to say 'maybe'.

"Let me guess, the coach picked you up while you were still sleeping, and you took a beating?"

So, there are no secrets on this campus?

It's my turn to scowl. I turn towards the room and meet Emily's gaze, which seems to be watching me curiously. I try to ignore her and look away, well aware that I'm not helping my case with this asshole attitude. And yet, God knows, at this moment I feel like ogling her.

"Yeah... He lectured me and excluded me from today's training. The team's in your hands," I reply, raising my eyebrows.

"You know he's right, Liam."

I groan loudly.

"Don't you start too! I thought we were friends!"

He smiles.

"Your grades have to come first if you want to succeed in school. You can rank well this year and hope to attract agents for the NHL draft. But you know that's not your future either.

What are you going to do if no team wants you? You're good. Hell, yeah... But you're not going to be a pro hockey player forever either."

I know he's saying it for my own good, like our coach, but right now I don't want to hear it.

"It's okay, Chase. Can we change the subject?"

He raises his hands in surrender and serves me something to fill my belly.

We chat for a while longer until I wolf down my breakfast and get ready to leave. I notice that Emily is gone.

Disappointment creeps into my chest, which irritates me a bit. I've got better things to do than think about this girl, who isn't my kind of girl at all.

Before I leave, Chase stops me and hands me a stack of papers.

"My course notes. Since you don't have any plans this afternoon, you can make up what you missed and return them to me this evening," he says with a wink.

"Oh, Chase, you didn't have to do that!" I reply sarcastically, leaving him to his customers.

Back in my room, I toss the papers unenthusiastically onto my desk. Yes, I should probably go through them and get ready for the next exam... But jogging around campus suddenly seems more fun.

Like an automaton, I slip on my running shoes and head out the door. Learning can wait!

The steady sound of my footsteps on the asphalt has a soothing effect and I can feel the fog dissipating in my head. But it's Emily's face that superimposes itself on my thoughts. Sitting by the window, laughing with her friend, her blue eyes were literally glowing. Her blond hair begging to be held in one hand, her greedy mouth destined for a kiss, or more...

Fuck, I'm going off the rails. I'm getting a boner just thinking about that little journalist!

I try to shake it out of my head. As this doesn't help, I increase my running speed, and finally, my salacious thoughts escape.

Back at the dorm, I'm completely out of breath. But I feel liberated and slightly exhausted. All I need now is a hot shower, and I can get down to the lessons Chase has been giving me.

Sitting at my desk, I stare at the pile of papers. It all looks like Chinese to me. Damn it... I'm in big trouble... Maybe a few snippets will stick in my brain if I just copy it down?

I grab a pen and look at the clock. Training started a while ago and I feel out of place just sitting at my desk. I just want to be on the ice right now... If I can't do what I love, I feel incomplete.

Pissed off, I head for the fridge and grab a beer. I can't even call one of my buddies, as they're all on their skates. Resigned, I pull out my cell phone and call my mom. We may not have the best relationship in the world, but somehow, she knows how to be there when I need her.

"Liam, shouldn't you be at practice?" she asks immediately, sighing.

"Hi, Mom, I'm fine, thanks for asking. How are you and my wonderful sisters?" I answer in my most innocent tone.

"What have you done now?" she insists.

"Nothing at all! The coach just wanted me to stop today so I could concentrate on my studies, because I've got exams coming up."

A little white lie.

There is a short silence.

"Well, I'm relieved. I thought something had happened."

We chat for a while longer and I notice that I'm starting to feel a little better. My mother has always had a way of triggering a feeling of well-being in me that makes all the dark clouds disappear. There's only one subject we avoid at all costs: my professional future. She's not a big fan of the fact that I want to pursue a career in ice hockey. And since discussions on this subject always end in an argument, we don't talk about it anymore.

When there's a sudden knock on my door, I put an end to our conversation and get up to open the door. Before me stands Chase with a black eye. I burst out laughing and let him in.

"I forbid you to say anything," he says.

He heads for the freezer of my little fridge, and pulls out a bag of frozen peas. It's essential for athletes like us to always have these on hand. Then he throws himself onto the sofa. Smiling, I pour him a beer and sit down next to him to toast.

After a moment's silence, he finally speaks.

"Training without you sucks!"

To which I respond by laughing out loud again.

"Sorry, man! Won't happen again."

We stay a while, enjoying the familiar silence.

Chase and I have been friends since kindergarten. He's like a brother to me. We've been through so much together and can count on each other one hundred percent. His bisexuality hasn't been easy for him to deal with, especially in the 'sports world', but I support him 100% and would break the bones of anyone who picked on him because he likes men as much as women. We're past that these days, and everyone should focus on their own desires. I know that in return, he'll always have my back.

"At practice, there was a pretty blonde looking for you. Have you been breaking hearts again?" he suddenly asks, waggling his eyebrows.

My heart beats a little faster, but I don't let on.

"What size bra?" I ask, looking deceptively casual.

Chase rolls his eyes.

"Blonde, blue eyes, pretty smile, hot. Sound familiar?"

I pretend to think, even though I know exactly who it is. And deep down, I can't help but be delighted that she came looking for me.

"Ah, yes, Emily. She's from the student newspaper and she's going to write several articles about us this season."

Chase nods and looks at me skeptically. I know I can't get away with my terseness in front of him. After so many years of friendship, I'm an open book to him.

"You're interested in her, man."

"What? No! She's not my type at all. She seems uptight. And what did she say to you?"

I keep a detached air. Chase laughs and pats me on the shoulder.

"I know you, Liam! When was the last time you had any real fun, huh?"

"Last weekend, thank you so much for worrying about my sex life," I reply, annoyed.

Chase raises his hands in defense.

"Anyway, she doesn't look like a one-night stand, if you ask me," he adds. "And yeah, Coach was clear about that, we need to ease up on the extras."

"It's true that you're not defeated, man!"

"I can't complain. But I'm going to class, so Franklyn's giving me a break. You should try it," he retorts.

Touché.

When he gets up to leave, he thanks me for the beer, and I take the opportunity to give him back his notes.

"I only understood a third of it, but thanks all the same," I say with an imperturbable smile.

He just nods, throws me the packet of peas he had on his

eye and leaves.

Alone again, I turn on the TV and flick between channels until I discover an old action movie. I make myself comfortable and immerse myself in another world.

At some point, I wake up, feeling cold and it's pitch-black outside. I yawn and stretch before lying down in bed. Falling asleep with a distraction is so much easier than waiting for sleep with my thoughts running in circles.

★★★

"It's good to see you on your feet so early in the morning!" exclaims Chase, intercepting me halfway to the classroom building and walking beside me.

After a refreshing shower, a cup of coffee and a muffin, I felt ready for class. If I'm honest, the coach's admonitions and the fact that I didn't get to train were also enough to motivate me. Today, I'm even enjoying the morning sunshine and fresh air, something I haven't had the chance to do in a while.

"Dude, are you escorting me or what? Are you afraid I'm going to run off?" I ask my best friend skeptically.

"Some people would kill to have a bodyguard that well groomed!" he retorts cheerfully.

Once in class, the teachers' monologues seem incredibly long and I can't wait to get out onto the ice.

The professor wakes me from my half-sleep with a question to which I have no answer. A few students laugh until Chase saves me and whispers what to say. I nod my thanks.

I'll never be a model student. My talent is on the ice. If I didn't need this damn diploma to ensure a 'future' and never miss another training session, I'd certainly be somewhere else. That's for sure.

An eternity later, the torture is finally over. Chase and I

meet up with the rest of the team for lunch in the refectory before heading off to train. We chat animatedly and joke around together.

I love these weekly lunches together. It's like an informal sports get-together. The family atmosphere and camaraderie are good for me. It's a bit like everyone else, given that we're away from our loved ones for the most part. We've become a family in our own way. Crude, with a dubious sense of humor, and a little alcoholic on the side.

When I'm finally on my skates, I feel complete again. I breathe in the cold air and savor the sensation of my feet gliding along without a hitch. Immediately, and very paradoxically, given the rather frigid setting, I burn with an inner fire.

During training, just as I'm about to catch a puck from one of my teammates, a mass of blond hair catches my eye. I inevitably raise my head and look for the silhouette, missing the pass that was holding out my arms.

"Damn it, Liam! What the hell are you doing?"

I grimace.

"Captain, you're screwing up!" adds one of the guys.

"Yeah, all right, I get it! Sorry, guys!" I reply, more annoyed with myself than with their well-deserved remarks.

I look at Chase, who merely observes me, raising his eyebrows. I look away and note, disappointed, that it's not even Emily standing there on the edge of the bleachers, ogling us.

Shit, this girl's gonna make me lose my shit...

I regain my composure and concentrate on the game. I score one goal after another to make up for my indiscretion.

Once the workout's over, Chase approaches me, laughing.

"Not your kind of journalist, eh?"

"Shut the fuck up," I say curtly and head for the locker room.

As usual, Coach Franklyn comes over to give us his speech.

"Not bad, guys, but you can do better. Liam, whatever it is that's on your mind, leave it at home next practice, please. There's no room on the ice for that kind of distraction."

"Yes, coach. It won't happen again," I growl before heading for the shower.

The hot water helps to calm me down a bit, but I'm still annoyed with myself when I set off for my room.

I need to find a way to put Emily out of my mind. Sleeping with her might be the answer, don't you think? A smirk stretches my lips.

Liam, you're such a jerk...

***

In the early hours of the morning, I still feel exhausted when my alarm goes off. Yet I force myself to get up and face the day.

Somehow Coach Franklyn and Chase are right. I need to improve my grades, especially if it means I can have a solid record and prove to recruiters that I'm serious. Who better than a player who knows how to manage his athletic life and his student life?

It's just that yesterday, I checked the NHL players' diplomas, and it's no joke. These guys have a lot on their minds, as well as being pretty damn good on the ice. Just look at John Hayden[3], my idol, who has a degree in political science, from Yale University no less.

Don't fall flat on your face, man. You can do it!

On my way to the campus cafeteria to get my usual coffee and muffin, I trip over a blond boy. More precisely, I bump into him, overlooking only his head.

---

3 With a degree in political science from Yale University, he played for the Chicago Blackhawks and Arizona Coyotes.

"Oh, sorry!" resounds a timid voice.

"No problem," I reply, lowering my eyes.

The rest of my repartee gets stuck in my throat: Emily stands before me, her cheeks rosy and her eyes bright.

"I... No worries, yeah..." I end up mumbling before quickly walking away.

Before her blue eyes captivate me, and I fall into them like *Alice in Wonderland*[4] down the white rabbit hole. It takes a lot of strength not to turn around.

That's anything but good.

As I arrive at the lecture hall, where I'm supposed to take one of my morning lectures, I notice that a few students have a newspaper in hand. A few of them give me unobtrusive glances, and wave with their chins, rather warmly.

I guess the article about our game is finally out, and from the reactions, it looks positive. I'm curious to know what Emily has written about us, and I manage to get one of the papers by retrieving it from the hands of a girl. I quickly settle down and look for the section about us.

My heart beats a little faster when I find the right page. I start reading and find myself doing it in one go. The article is incredibly well written! Emily has captured the essence of our sport and team spirit perfectly. I can't even hear the teacher start; I'm so captivated by her words. She really has talent. And for once, there's no scandal on the horizon. If I didn't love hockey, I think I'd be tempted to go and see a game, and that's a really good thing!

I find it hard to follow the rest of the course. I read and reread the article, transported by the little blonde's prose. It goes to show that, in addition to having a great ass, she knows how to write.

When I get to the rink, the atmosphere is happy and re-

---

[4] Fantasy novel by British author Lewis Carroll, published in 1865.

laxed. The guys all tap me on the shoulder as if in gratitude.

"I don't know what you told that blonde girl last time, but her article is brilliant!" says Tyler, our defender.

"If the stands aren't full by the next game, I'll eat my stick!" exclaims Eliot, the goalkeeper.

"No one can resist my charm," I joke.

That's when Coach Franklyn enters the locker room and chases us all out onto the ice.

"Enough chatter! You'll remake the world when you're dripping with sweat, not before! We've got a lot of work to do. Go, go, go!"

I scan the hall briefly, perhaps expecting to find our journalist. After all, she was looking for me last time, yet she hasn't come back... Maybe she's found the answers to her questions? Silly me, I should have given her my phone number. Or I could have stalked her on Instagram... It would have been a good excuse to contact her again. 'Hey, Emily! I heard you were looking for me, if you feel like chatting over a strawberry milk, I'm in...' Fuck, I'm rambling! She did a pro job; now it's my turn to do mine. If she's drawn attention to us, we've got to earn it twice as much.

Chase appears behind me and pats me on the back.

"She's not here, brother, it's no use waiting for her like a faithful dog!"

I growl and slap him back. It annoys me so much that he can see right through me like that!

An hour later, a shrill whistle echoes through the air, bringing our warm-up to an end. Panting, I glide across the ice. With each energetic step, the blades of my skates raise icy flakes around my feet.

The coach shouts his orders and we split into two teams. I look at my teammates with pride: these guys are good. As captain, I must be even more so.

Sweat and effort are forgotten as soon as the puck comes into play. With stoic concentration, I get into position, my eyes firmly fixed on the opposing goal. Adrenalin pulses through my veins. Then another whistle blows and we're instantly in a trance. I glide like a feather to retrieve the puck at lightning speed. Only one thing matters now: getting the attack on goal. But my opponents don't make it easy. After a few passes, I find the weak point in their game and slip through their defense. Joy breaks out when the puck hits the net, marking my team's first point.

I smile at my teammates and bang my stick against Chase's. It's our way of celebrating a point. But the exercise isn't over yet. I quickly get back into position, ready for the next attack.

When the final whistle blows and I take off my helmet, I'm dripping with sweat. My brown curls are a mess. I push the damp locks out of my eyes before I spot Emily standing next to Coach Franklyn. They seem to be deep in conversation and, as I approach, they both ignore me. Emily finally thanks the coach and leaves the room without a glance at me. To say I'm disappointed would be a lie. I'm fucking disappointed, yeah!

I tilt my head to the side, puzzled, and watch her walk away. At no point does she turn around.

I frown.

This is the first time I've ever been ghosted by a girl. But the truth is, I had it coming. If every time I meet her, I pretend she doesn't exist, it's only natural that she'll return the favor. Am I indulging in a little game of seduction? Come on... It won't hurt anyone... And after all, if I manage to get what's been haunting my nights for days, maybe she'll finally come out of my dreams!

3

Emily

I've been chatting to Coach Franklyn for a while now, when he finally blows the whistle on the end of the hockey team's practice. With a keen eye, he follows their progress while talking to me about the upcoming season's games. My article was appreciated, and I'm glad it was. The feedback was so good that I was asked to follow the team within the editorial team. I'm good at getting a seat in the stands at every game! But it's the lesser of two evils, and I'm especially glad that my efforts and research have paid off! For someone who didn't understand the sport two weeks ago...

When Liam approaches us, sweaty and above all terribly sexy, my heart misses a beat.

It's the stereotypical student athlete, let's face it. Maddie and Cassy were right when they warned me to beware of these specimens. But God, he's handsome! It's indecent. And I bet he's all muscle under that jersey...

That said, on the rare occasions we crossed paths, he ignored me as if we'd never spoken. I could almost feel the ice coldness he excels at swirling around him. As if our conversation had never happened. And yet, I'm not crazy, he made a pass at me! But then, flirting must be like a second sport for him, just as easy as the first... Maybe his attitude was also just a front to get him featured in my article. Anyway, it's not the first time I've been fooled by a guy.

You need to toughen up, Emily!

I decide without hesitation to avoid him and don't even glance at him. It would be too much honor for the gentleman! It's obvious that he's just looking for good publicity on my back. And he's probably the big asshole I've heard described several times. In any case, it's no secret on campus that he doesn't let any conquest pass him by as soon as it gets a little close to his nets. Well, I won't be fooled!

It's probably best to avoid unnecessary encounters whenever possible. I don't want to be one of those girls who runs after him drooling, and I'm not interested in an arrogant guy like him either. Our collaboration will stop at the weekly articles I have to write about the ice hockey team.

Leaving the rink, I head straight for my room, which Cassy is redecorating once again. From the way I close the door before slumping onto our little sofa, she knows something's wrong. Head bent; she watches me curiously.

"Do you want to talk about it?"

"No," I reply, resigned.

"All right."

She simply shrugs and goes back to decorating. After a while, she brings me a cup of tea. It's exactly what I need, and I thank her with a small smile, suddenly a little embarrassed to have turned her down.

Without saying a word, she sits down next to me. Which is rather unusual for her. Not that she's normally a chatterbox, but... yes... Cassy is a *real* chatterbox! It's certainly fun and comforting, but sometimes, it's also very tiring.

After a short silence, she finally speaks up, as if the quiet in our room is too much for her to bear.

"Whatever's bothering you, it'll pass. And you're not alone."

I simply nod and take a big sip from my cup. The taste is mild and goes very well with the honey.

I feel my tension release.

"I know what you need!" Cassy suddenly says, excitedly.

I look at her quizzically.

"A shopping spree! There's this new vintage store opening this weekend. You and Maddie absolutely must come!"

While I can think of several things that would cheer me up, running around the stores isn't one of them. But her excitement is almost contagious, and I have to admit that since I've been sharing her room, Cassy has been a pretty good friend. She's always in a cheerful mood, and even though she talks a lot, she's interesting.

But there's an important hockey game this weekend and I have to write about it. That means I still have to see Liam Scott and watch him, for several hours. Handsome, fresh, athletic, hot, sexy... In short. Torture.

I inhale and exhale deeply.

On the other hand, the distraction offered by Cassy could do me good and take my mind off things, as well as getting me off campus. So far, I haven't had a chance to go and see what's out there outside my course buildings, and the university newspaper. Besides the skating rink, of course. So, the opportunity seems nice, and I end up accepting.

What could go wrong? Maybe I'll even find a great outfit to complete my wardrobe, which Cassy finds too conservative for her taste.

My roommate can hardly contain her enthusiasm and kisses me on the cheek before leaping to her feet and leaping joyfully across the room.

"We're finally going to be able to find you some decent clothes," she gloats with a big smile.

"My clothes are fine! I don't want to look like..."

I stop instantly when Cassy raises an eyebrow, waiting for the next part. I don't want to offend her.

"Like what?"

"Vintage clothes don't suit everyone," I say.

"Oh, honey... There's nothing wrong with your clothes, you know, it's just that they don't make you look your best."

I grimace and concentrate on my mug of tea.

The next morning, I cautiously open my eyes to see what time it is. Clearly too early. But I've got a lot to do today, and I can't ignore the minutes any longer, or I'll end up being late.

Hoping that a shower might help me wake up for good, I drag myself to the bathroom, grumbling.

The warm water feels good on my shoulders and neck. I hadn't realized how tense I was. My subconscious must be overwhelmed by all the new challenges ahead.

Maybe I should start the day with a bit of yoga... After all, it relaxes the body and the mind. But before I can imagine myself doing the figure of the dog sitting facing the rising sun, I've already decided it's a bad idea. Might as well leave it to the really flexible. Me, I'd just pull a muscle.

When I leave the bathroom, Cassy is already drinking her coffee. Without a word - she seems to be respecting my need for morning silence more and more - she passes me a freshly brewed one.

"Are you feeling better this morning?" she asks, peering over the rim of her cup.

I take a deep sip before answering.

"Now that caffeine is coursing through my veins, yes."

We both laugh.

"Would you like to come to the gym with me this morning?" asks Cassy.

I look at her doubtfully.
Well, a little jog never killed anyone, right?
"Why not, yes!"
"Namaste!" she says simply, handing me her cup of coffee to toast with.

My mouth opens and closes. It seems she wasn't suggesting I just go for a run.
Rha shit... What am I getting myself into...
We finish our coffee and get ready.

Cassy sports all the accessories of a true yogi, while I... well, I throw on the best I have on hand to prevent my pants from tearing at the butt: black leggings and a loose-fitting tee.

The yoga studio on campus is still fairly empty in the early morning. The first class with yoga teacher Lara starts at 7:30. It's supposed to help participants start the day positive and full of energy. But it seems that Cassy and I are the only yogis today, fresh and ready enough to open our chakras.

Lara enters the room with a warm smile and greets us with a friendly "Namaste".

We begin the class with breathing exercises, with soft, relaxing music playing in the background. I can't help but think of Maddie and how silly she would find this, which completes the stretching of a silly smile on my face.

We do a few fairly accessible yoga poses - fortunately - and finish with more breathing exercises.

At the end of the class, I watch Cassy out of the corner of my eye, who seems to be in a deep trance. She's sitting gracefully in a lotus position with her eyes closed. At the sound of the gong, she slowly opens them and looks at me in amazement.

"What?" she asks, clearing her throat.

I start laughing.

"I've never seen you so calm and relaxed!"

"Oh, I'm quite multifaceted," she replies with a shrug.

I conceal a smile, and once the mats have been put away, we thank Lara before leaving the studio.

"Coffee! And preferably intravenous," I moan.

I'm much more flexible than when I woke up, but I still don't feel perfectly awake. It has to be said that such a quiet time before starting the day, personally, makes me feel rather sleepy.

Cassy just laughs and puts her arm around my shoulders.

"We should probably reward ourselves with a waffle too!" she says.

"The best idea of the day!"

We go to the campus bar and place our order.

Behind the counter, the handsome barista on duty calls out to me.

"You're Emily, right?"

"Yes..." I answer, surprised that this guy knows my first name.

"My name's Chase! I play on the hockey team with Liam Scott," he explains as he prepares our order.

"Nice to meet you, Chase," I exclaim. "And this is my roommate Cassy," I say as Cassy digs her elbow into my ribs and clears her throat.

"Hi," she says confidently.

Am I dreaming or is she batting her eyelashes?

"Will that be all?" asks Chase.

He hands us our cappuccinos and seems captivated by Cassy.

"We'll have two waffles with that, please," I say, breaking eye contact between the two of them.

"Coming right up," says Chase, getting down to work.

So, he plays on the same team as the arrogant team captain... I should have known. But with their helmets on, it's hard to recognize them off the ice.

Chase hands us the still-warm pastries and we pay.

"Thanks again for your article, Emily. The whole team liked it. Especially Liam, to tell the truth."

I can feel the red slowly creeping up my cheeks.

What the hell! So, I'm incapable of behaving myself when people talk to me about this guy. What do I care if he liked my article? I didn't write it for him!

"You're welcome. It's my job," I assert to calm my hormones and appear detached.

With drinks and waffles in hand, we head back to our room. On the way, Cassy can't stop raving about Chase. She describes every tiny detail of his face as if it were a poem. I just laugh at her remarks.

Once we've had breakfast, I change quickly. Today, I want to go to the library to study. In a quiet, studious atmosphere, I'll certainly be able to concentrate better than at the café, or even here, away from the chatter of my lovely roommate. I've got lessons to study and I still need to work on my hockey knowledge.

The path leading to the library is lined with trees and little benches in the sun. It almost makes you want to stop there, but I give in to temptation, telling myself I'd be more comfortable sitting at a table. I'd also be able to fall asleep and wake up three hours later…

Once in the building in question, I find a secluded table and get down to work. Media law is not my strong point, but it's a really important subject for understanding the legal and ethical aspects of my future profession.

Fortunately, the library is rather empty. I don't like working when there's too many people around. I always feel uncomfortable. Here, I can concentrate to my heart's content and pile up all the documentation I want in front of me. Because, yes, when it comes to research, I'm rather old school, and I like to go straight to the books for information, rather than the Internet.

After an hour of intense concentration, as I stifle a yawn, my gaze is drawn to the opening and closing of the automatic door. My heartbeat quickens instantly as Liam Scott enters.

What the hell is he doing here?

Our eyes meet briefly before I turn away to dive back into my book, silently hoping that he'll ignore me, as he has so far. Even as his heavy footsteps approach, I keep my eyes downcast.

To my surprise, a shadow looms over me and I deduce that he has stopped right in front of my table.

"Emily," he murmurs.

The sound of my first name coming out of his mouth feels like a caress on my skin. And I hate that feeling!

I clear my throat and finally look up at him. His blue gaze is intense, and I can see he's searching for his words to tell me something, but he doesn't seem to know where to start.

"Hi," I reply simply, trying to keep my voice even, even though my heart is racing.

Why does my body react to him in such an extreme way?

"Um... I'm sorry," he says, rubbing his face.

His words trouble me, but I look at him unimpressed.

"Sorry for what?"

A strange silence suddenly settles between us. I can feel my throat going dry and my hands are starting to sweat.

"For ignoring you," he finally says.

My jaw nearly drops, but I recover quickly.

"Ha... I hadn't noticed," I say as casually as possible, but my voice probably gives me away.

He gives me a puzzled look and turns on his heels without adding anything, leaving me like an idiot to watch his back as he walks away. When his footsteps are far enough away, I drop my head on the table.

What the hell was that?

I try to concentrate again, but it's impossible now. Frustrated, I gather my things and set off for my room.

Liam Scott has apologized! Because he wants another sensational article? Because the coach gave him a talking-to? Because he feels stupid given that I praised him in what I wrote? Because...

Rha... This sucks! This guy sucks!

The scene in the library keeps replaying in my mind. No one has ever had such an effect on me. Until now, I'd hoped it was just wounded pride because he was ignoring me. But now I find it hard to deny. My whole body seems to be reacting to Liam.

Crap.

I can't let him destabilize me like that. I've worked hard to get here and now I have to concentrate fully on my studies. Losing my mind over a guy doesn't really help. Not to mention that he's already been with half of the university.

The ringing of my phone pulls me out of my thoughts.

"Hey Maddie!" I say, taking the call and trying to sound 'normal'.

"Hi, beautiful! How are you? Am I interfering with your studies?" she asks mysteriously.

"Everything's fine! And no, I'm going back to the bedroom now."

"Oh, good, I'm outside your door!"

As I make my way back to my building and up to my floor, I catch a glimpse of her. She waves and we hang up. Then she greets me with a big kiss on the cheek.

"It's time to introduce you to New York nightlife. We're going out tonight! And I forbid you to say no!" she declares, pushing me towards the front door of my room.

"But... but Maddie... I... No! I really must..." I stammer.

"Shush! Tonight, there are no rules: we're going to have the time of our lives!"

Oh, my God! She sounds so serious when she says that that I start to panic. Where the hell is she going to drag me? No rules? Sounds like a debauched hangout to me!

"You're far too conscientious, my dear! Let someone who's been here a while tell you that. You always have to leave time for a little fun. Otherwise, you'll soon go crazy, you know!"

I look at her, a little unsettled.

"Just relax, Emily! I'm not taking you to some punk cave. It's just a buddy of mine, Tyler, who's throwing a party. A few guys and a lot of fun... Don't worry," explains my best friend, making her eyebrows dance in a knowing way.

With squinted eyes, I watch her. She's sold me this kind of party several times in the past, and it's never ended well.

I take a deep breath.

On the other hand, I need to distract myself after this strange encounter with Liam.

"Yeah..." I finally let go, which Maddie takes as a yes.

She bounces with joy.

From now on, there's no turning back. If Maddie's got it in her head that we're going out, we're going out. After all, she's waited a whole year for me to finally show up. So, I let myself be convinced for good.

By the end of the day, I'm all set. Cassy is also on board, which reassures me a little. Only a little, because she's gesticulating all over the place like this is the event of the century.

When I look in the mirror, I'm a little apprehensive. It has to be said that, in the tight-fitting - and very short - dress that Cassy and Maddie have imposed on me, I feel a little disguised. But after all, I live in New York, in the city that never sleeps and, incidentally, is very stylish! It's a new life, in which I can also reinvent myself.

We set off arm-in-arm to the waiting Uber. This takes us to an off-campus fraternity house where the famous Tyler lives. Him and his 'brothers', it seems. Because the car stops in front of a fairly large, modern house, teeming with people. Wide-eyed, I look around.

Damn, I'm about to go to my first student party!

Excited, I leave the car and follow my friends to the entrance, where small groups have already gathered. Maddie greets them as if she knows them all and beckons me to come closer.

"Attention, everyone! This is..." - she points at me with a sweeping gesture – "my best friend, Emily. She's new to the university and deserves a particularly warm welcome tonight!"

Well, obviously, she knows them all. Wow! In just one year, Maddie seems to have met quite a few people. She's simply amazing, and much more sociable than I am.

I awkwardly raise my hand in greeting before we rush into the house. As soon as we reach the front door, the music starts to play and I already know it's going to be an exciting night.

It's very crowded and we're having trouble finding our way around. The house is classy and unadorned, but at the moment it looks more like a giant bar. Several sofas are overflowing with people chatting, kissing or... outright groping each other.

I'd heard that university parties were very lively, but experiencing them live is something else entirely.

I let my gaze wander around the room and...

It can't be! Liam... This guy is everywhere!

My heart misses a beat and I turn instinctively, hoping he hasn't seen me. I tug nervously at my dress to try and hide my thighs, which I suddenly find too exposed.

Maddie hands me a Coke in front of my nose and I take an eager sip.

"You look like you've seen a ghost," she says, looking at me with concern.

"Just this stupid hockey player. But everything's fine," I reply.

This seems to satisfy her. After all, she has no idea about the very strange encounter between Liam and me. I haven't had time to explain it to her. She would have been able to push me towards him to try and clear things up.

As Cassy stands in front of me, soda in hand, we toast and Maddie leads us both onto the dance floor. Unconsciously, I look around for Liam, but I don't see him. Not that I don't feel like having fun tonight, but it makes me uncomfortable to know that he might be watching me from a corner of the room. I don't feel like exposing myself to this guy. I try to forget my ghostly vision and relax.

After a few songs, we get thirsty and head for the kitchen, where plenty of refreshments are on offer. Before we've had time to help ourselves, three young men approach us and hand us bottles of beer.

"Shake a leg with us girls, there's plenty to party about!" shouts one of them to drown out the sound of the music.

Maddie is the first to react. She accepts the bottles gratefully, observes them for a fraction of a second, and, satisfied with her inspection, finally uncaps them with a sure hand.

Rule number 1, my best friend told me, is to never accept open bottles or glasses from strangers. Yeah, you never know what they've put in them!

"What are we celebrating?" she asks.

The guys look us up and down before one of them answers.

"Your beauty!"

Icebound Attraction

What a cliché!

We just laugh, almost out of politeness, and toast. Maddie winks at me, discreetly pointing at the blond in front of me. She accompanies her maneuver with a nudge of her elbow. I roll my eyes and shake my head almost imperceptibly. She laughs out loud and raises her hands in apology.

After a little chat with our three flirts, which is far from interesting, Maddie drags us back onto the dance floor and, as always, she doesn't take 'no' for an answer. At least it gets us out of this kitchen!

Suddenly, I feel a hand on the small of my back. My whole body stiffens as someone whispers in my ear how much they'd like to help me take off my dress.

No, I'm dreaming! Feeling his breath on the back of my neck sends a chill down my spine and I try to free myself from his grip. Cassy observes the scene before slipping in between me and the obviously drunk man.

"You're wasting your time. She's mine," she says, hugging me.

"Thank you," I whisper.

But the drunk doesn't seem to want to leave his place. He soon reaches around Maddie to grab me by the arm and pull me close. Just then, Liam reappears in my field of vision. His eyes narrow when he sees me and his gaze settles on the guy's hand gripping my arm, rather forcefully. I must have the face of a girl who doesn't consent, because soon he approaches us and pulls the intruder by his shirt.

"Back off, Josh. They're with me."

"Oh, sorry, man! I thought that..."

"Stop thinking and go look somewhere else," he growls through gritted teeth.

The so-called Josh scratches his cheek contritely and scurries off. Liam then looks me up and down, and his face closes.

"No wonder people are sniffing around you in that outfit. That said, it suits you."

I open my mouth to say something back, but he's already walking away.

But what nerve!

Well, I should thank him too. He pulled me out of that other jerk's hands, but he's still a jerk too.

"What happened?" asks Cassy, who hasn't really grasped the situation.

Maddie shrugs in response, and I shake my head in turn.

"Nothing…"

My eyes search for Liam, but I don't see him.

"Is everything okay?" my roommate asks again.

"It's just that… This guy here was a bit too insistent, and Liam Scott just had him removed."

"Some of them have a knack for not knowing what the word 'no' means, or even seeming to understand when you don't want to be approached."

She sighs and raises her eyes to the sky.

"Let's get something to drink," says Maddie.

As I turn to leave the dance floor, I spot Liam with a pretty blonde. She's standing next to him, staring at him like she's about to devour him.

But… it's Lara, the yoga teacher! All that meditation, all that self-control, just to fall into the arms of the hockey team captain, renowned for being a real player? What a disappointment!

An unpleasant twinge runs through my stomach, but I ignore it. This is probably the first time I've seen him in his natural habitat. A hunter with his prey. And I find it rather unpleasant.

After another drink, Cassy and I dance some more, while Maddie has fun with a new conquest. My best friend really knows how to meet people!

After a while, as my gaze keeps wandering to Liam and Lara - which annoys me - I start to yawn. I'm not used to staying out this long. Tired, I tap my best friend on the shoulder and tell her I want to leave.

"You can go, I'm in good hands!" she retorts, embracing her dance partner.

I can't help but smile. Maddie always knew what she wanted and how to get it.

Cassy nods at me and together we make our way out. We put on our jackets and order an Uber. As I take one last look around, I just have time to see Liam and the yoga teacher disappear down the stairs, arm in arm.

I shake my head.

I groan and yawn when Cassy puts a cup of coffee under my nose the next morning.

"Hello, sunshine!" she exclaims a little too loudly for my taste.

She's far too cheerful for this early morning. I accept the cup and reach for my cell phone.

"It's 11 o'clock, if you must know," says Cassy. "And that's the perfect time to head to the new vintage store!"

I put my coffee down on my bedside table and let myself fall back on my cushion.

"Give me half an hour's respite," I beg, stretching for a long time.

Then there is a knock on the bedroom door.

"Hello, Maddie!" sings Cassy again, and Maddie jumps into bed with me.

She's wearing the same clothes as last night, smelling of smoke and alcohol. Clearly, she hasn't gone home yet.

"Maddie," I squeak out.

She laughs heartily and tickles me until I sit up for good.

"You've slept far too long," she says sternly, tossing me a pillow.

"I agree with her!" I hear Cassy exclaim from our little kitchen.

"You're really mean."

I trot to the bathroom, grumbling.

"And you're not a morning person,'" shouts Maddie behind me before more pillows fly against the door.

When I come out of the bathroom, they're sitting at the table and Maddie is recounting her crazy night, in far too much detail.

When they see me, they both exclaim:

"At last!"

"You really need new clothes," Cassy repeats to herself for what seems like the hundredth time.

I look in the mirror and sigh, resigned.

"Well, let's go..."

Cassy is excited and already clapping her hands. I really have to break her of this habit.

The idea of going to just one store soon turns into a frantic shopping spree. Just in time for me to go to the hockey game, even though I'm exhausted and just want to go to bed!

I throw my bags on the bed and am about to leave when Cassy stops me.

"You've got great clothes now; don't you want to dress up a bit?"

She waves her eyebrows defiantly.

It's true that I like the outfits she helped me choose today, and I feel pretty good in them. But I don't want to be late either. I look at the bags, then at my watch, and decide to change quickly. Skinny jeans, boots and a low-cut sweater are enough to satisfy my roommate and make me look presentable, according to her.

The rink is really packed for this game. Coach Franklyn stands as always on the bench, an expert eye on his players. I join him and settle down with some notes. He greets me with a nod, while the teams are already assembled on the ice.

I meet Liam's gaze and he dares to wink at me. I ignore my racing heartbeat and quickly look down at my notebook. He'd better concentrate on his opponents!

At the first whistle, the players rush onto the ice. I have to admit that the captain is once again in top shape - his technique is impeccable. He controls the puck with his stick and deftly dribbles past the defenders. His teammates position themselves in support, ready to take over, if need be, but Liam only has eyes for the opposing goal. With a swift movement on his skates, he skates around the goalkeeper and the puck flies into the net.

Shouts are flying all around us. The stadium is in an uproar, but I try to keep an eye on the team. For them, there's no pause, and they barely celebrate the point they've scored before continuing to slide up and down the rink. However, I notice that Liam's face is lit up and his eyes shine with contentment. He really is an outstanding player. Even I, as a beginner, can't help but recognize that. It wouldn't be surprising if sports agents were scrambling to recruit him and try to pick him up at the next draft[5].

After the final whistle, our university's victory is overwhelming. The players are euphoric, banging their sticks together. The coach also seems to be jubilant, along with the crowd, who are shouting their joy. After a while, Liam approaches me and gives me a warm smile. I hate feeling my whole body tingle just because he smiles at me. But I need another interview

---

[5] Every year, NHL teams select eligible players in the entry draft.

for my new article, so I put aside my confusion to get up and meet him.

"Nice game," I say casually. "Can I ask you a few more questions for the paper?"

"Of course! That's what we agreed on anyway."

Well, if we've agreed then...

I pout a little, and he heads for the door that allows players to exit the rink. Comfortable on his skates, he trots over to my bench and sits down. I try to keep a reasonable distance from him, but I'm close enough to see drops of sweat beading from his hair as he removes his helmet.

This guy is *really* hot.

I have to focus!

As I ask my questions and write down his answers, he keeps staring at me. Uncomfortable to feel his blue eyes on me, I waddle in my seat. From time to time, I look up and meet his gaze. I curse myself for blushing so easily! His slightly curved nose, his full lips... everything is a call to lust. I realize this, and it pisses me off. I do my best to focus on his athletic performance, but despite myself, I retain every detail of his face. His few freckles, an uneven scar on his chin, the brown curls that fall over his face. His muscular physique fits in well with it all.

Emily! Be professional!

Suddenly, I realize I haven't really been listening to what he's just said, and I clear my throat. Does he know the effect he's having on women? The effect he has on me? I quickly look away and pretend to look at my notes.

"Maybe we should continue this conversation over a drink," he suggests. "It's not that I don't enjoy it, far from it, but I really need to shower."

All at once, I come to. Although I'm finding it harder and harder to resist his charm, I let out a tense smile.

"Thanks, but I've got everything I need!" I reply defensively.

He just smiles and shrugs.

We stand up at the same time, and I almost trip over him. He holds me by the arm before I crash into him. His grip is firm and his smell is absolutely delicious, even though he's just sweated for hours. A mixture of cedar wood and spices.

I'm completely delirious! I've got to get out of here.

"Ahem, sorry..."

"It's nothing."

He releases me and I stand up, trying to gather my dignity.

"Well, see you next time," he blows a little too close to my ear, and I get goose bumps.

We look into each other's eyes briefly, his face so close to mine that my knees buckle.

Now I absolutely can't deny it: I'm very attracted to him.

Fuck it.

I don't want to be a name on his 'fuck list'. And from what I saw at the previous party, Liam likes to flirt, and score goals.

4

Liam

I know I've just played with fire. I know it... Her face was so close to mine that it would have only taken a small impulse on my part to kiss her. I had to pull myself together and remember where we were, in addition to who she is: the journalist who's supposed to make me shine. Nothing more. And yet, I can't ignore the fact that she's on my mind more and more.

Her big eyes are the color of a lagoon, her blond hair frames her delicious face and her lips... Fuck... If I keep going, I'll get a hard-on!

I turn away from her and head for the changing rooms. My whole body protests. Emily unleashes a desire in me that I've never felt before.

Maybe because she's untouchable? At the same time, I'm the one stopping myself... Do I find pleasure in telling myself that she's 'forbidden'? Does holding back turn me on?

Shit, I'm getting kinky...

But I can't ignore the fact that the coach wouldn't like it at all. And he's right: I have to concentrate on hockey. This girl isn't a one-night stand, I keep telling myself, and I'm convinced of it. If I slip, I've got a feeling it won't just be for one night. She's the kind of girl you want to come back to. I'm convinced of it every time I get a little closer. But I can't ignore the fact that I like the effect I seem to have on her. Because yes, I'm not blind, and even if she protests and seems to push me away, there's a little something that makes me believe she's not totally insensitive to my charm.

Does that make you feel better, you big moron?

Yeah, I have to admit, my manhood is happy about it. But my dick is still hungry. Charming, eh?

The next morning, I'm startled by a loud bang and immediately fall back onto my pillow. My head is buzzing. I'd had quite a few beers yesterday... In trying to forget the object of my fantasies, I'd celebrated our victory a little too much.

When there's another knock at the door, I force myself out of bed. I hope it's not important. No sooner have I opened the door than Chase bursts in.

"Hello to you too, Chase, come on in and make yourself at home," I growl.

He laughs.

"Dude, it's 9 o'clock. I was sure you'd slept through your alarm, so you can thank me! You've got to hurry, we've got to get to class. Besides, you look like shit."

I frown.

"Fuck you," I say, snarling again.

"Looks like someone's got a hangover," Chase jokes.

I roll my eyes.

"Let me take a quick shower and inject some caffeine into my bloodstream, then we can get going. Yes, I'm hurrying!" I exclaim, rushing into the bathroom.

Chase throws himself on the couch and taps on his phone while I get ready.

After a shower and a large glass of Coke, I feel a little better and we're off.

A day at school should take my mind off things. My thoughts keep wandering to Emily and it's annoying me. Although I've made a firm resolution to concentrate on ice hockey, I can't stop thinking about her. It doesn't help that our meetings don't leave her indifferent either.

After class, I'm a bit depressed. My major is hard to understand and I have trouble following the teacher's explanations.

On the way back, I pass the café hoping Chase will be on duty to cheer me up. But he doesn't seem to be there.

I order a coffee and a sandwich before sitting down in a corner. I don't usually pay much attention to who's there, but this time I can't ignore my surroundings - Emily is sitting at a table nearby, engrossed in her notebook.

My feet seem to have a life of their own, as I head straight for her. When she notices me, she looks up and an expression of surprise, tinged with uncertainty, passes over her face before she hides it behind a neutral smile.

"Hi, Liam," she says, closing her notebook.

Without asking permission, I sit down next to her. For a guy who promised to ignore her...

"How are you?" I ask, a little awkwardly, trying to get the conversation going.

"I'm fine," she replies soberly, stirring her tea. "I've just written the draft of your article for the newspaper and I'm preparing my next subject."

I should probably read between the lines and leave her alone; she obviously has a lot to do. But my body won't obey me.

"Sounds great," I reply, not really knowing what else to say.

At that moment, I just don't want to go and leave her. I also have to admit that she comes alive when she talks about her work, and that makes her hotter. It's really hard to avoid her when she attracts me like a walking magnet. I know I wanted to distance myself, but now that I'm face-to-face with her, I have no intention of doing so.

"In any case, it's a pleasure to write about your team. You're in excellent shape so far," she continues. "Well, especially you, you're really good."

She dares a smile.

This unexpected compliment gives me a warm feeling. I force myself to suppress this emotion with difficulty.

"Thank you, Emily. You do a great job with your articles too. Readers love them, and we did notice a bigger crowd at our last game. It's cool to have encouragement when you're playing."

She smiles gratefully, but I can sense that she's still on the fence. Everything in me wants to break down the wall between us, but I'm afraid of what will happen if I get too close to her. It's as if we're both part of a masquerade not to show what really touches us.

It doesn't make sense!

I stand up abruptly.

"Have a good day."

She looks a little lost and just nods.

I return to my table and the waiter brings me my sandwich. As I take my first bite, I watch Emily, sitting with her back to me.

There's definitely something between us that I can't ignore, no matter how hard I try. But I have to be careful. My dream of joining the NHL is at stake. Coach Franklyn has told us often enough about former team members who were destined for great things but got distracted by 'love'.

His words, not mine. Liam Scott has never been in love, and he's not about to be!

How's it going, man, talking about yourself in the third person?

Up until now, I'd always stuck to a little sex - well, sometimes a lot - with my conquests, but then our paths would separate. No selfies together, no romantic breakfasts, no trips together, no introductions to parents, or even friends. Nothing. Just well-rehearsed sex plans to make the evenings and days seem shorter. Besides, feelings are annoying. They make you weak, and if you let them into your life once, you're done for! All the women I met agreed with that, as far as I could tell. If they weren't, at least none of them ever complained about it out loud.

However, when I look at Emily, I wonder how long I'll be able to ignore my attraction to her. Inwardly, I berate myself. I need to prioritize and control myself.

Suddenly, I feel like I can't breathe. I abandon my half-eaten sandwich and practically run out of the café. I need some fresh air.

There are too many people on campus and everything revolves around me. Unable to think clearly, I jog home and close the door. Once inside, I lean against it, breathing in and out deeply.

What the hell is happening to me?

Without thinking, I go into the bathroom and run cold water over my hands. It calms my nerves and, after a few minutes, my breathing becomes regular again.

Once I've calmed down, I notice I'm late for training. Franklyn won't like me arriving when everyone's already warmed up.

I grab my gym bag and rush out the door. But even on the double, I'm ten minutes late.

As expected, the coach gives me a stern look.

"Sorry, I forgot the time when I was studying," I lie.

"Don't let it become a habit! Off to the ice," he says coldly.

I focus and it helps me forget my little panic attack. It's like entering another world when I'm on my skates.

After training, Coach Franklyn invites me into his office.

"Are you ready for tomorrow's exam?" he asks, slightly worried.

Holy shit! I completely forgot about this exam.

"Uh, yes..." I say uncertainly.

He breathes a sigh of relief. He obviously believes me.

"Good to hear! Good luck Liam," he says, letting me go.

Once again, I rush home. I throw my bag in the corner and immediately sit down at my desk. I frantically rummage through my papers until I find the material I'll be tested on tomorrow. And I can't understand a word I'm reading. Yet I try to concentrate and learn it all by heart.

When my eyes start to burn, I throw the documents on the table, resigned, and go to bed. Why do I have such a hard time getting myself to study and get good grades outside of sports? I'm no dumber than anyone else, but it just won't go in! With my thoughts racing, I go to bed, unsure of what's going to happen tomorrow.

★★★

Nervous and tired at the same time, I sit in the examination room and struggle to keep my leg still. A student turns to me and glares. Some of the questions aren't that difficult and I manage to answer them. But as for the rest, I can't do a thing...

I leave my office early and, once I've handed in my copy, I walk into the campus park, frustrated. Business isn't my thing. My future manager will take care of everything for me.

I sigh.

In spite of everything, I have to finish my studies with good grades. Hell, I can do it! I've got the motivation to do it, I've got to keep going.

In the days that follow, I try to reconcile my training program with my academic obligations. I stay up until midnight every night to study for tests and exams. But very quickly, my tiredness has a negative impact on my athletic performance.

Once again, Coach Franklyn summons me to his office. It's almost becoming a habit these days.

"You look tired, Liam. Is everything all right?"

"Perfectly all right, Coach. I studied late last night, that's all," I reply sincerely.

"If you need time to study, you can also skip training for a few days," he suggests.

"No way, coach! If I don't train, I might not get drafted," I protest.

"You have to find a better balance. You can't go on like this. Please try to get organized. Something that will help, without burning you out. Maybe you need a tutor for your classes? Think about it."

I sigh and leave his office. I feel like I'm sinking into an abyss, and I don't know how I'm going to get out of it. The responsibility of being team captain and achieving my goals at university is weighing heavily on me.

When I get to my room, I sit down in front of my laptop and log on to the exam portal. The results are due to be announced today. I take a deep breath and close my eyes before reopening them and clicking on the result.

Failed the exam. Of course."

It's not surprising, but I'm still upset. It's hard to breathe again and I'm desperate to move. I just want to slide on the ice and not think about anything.

"That's enough stress for today," I decide, gathering my things.

Fortunately, the rink is empty. Just what I need. I grab a few pucks and practice shooting at the goal. Absorbed in my frustration, I don't even notice that Chase has entered the ice. When I turn around, he's skating towards me.

"Hey, man!" he throws at me.

"Hi," I reply briefly.

"Stressed?" he asks.

"What, do I look stressed?"

He just looks at me. Chase knows me too well. He knows when I don't feel like talking. We line up a few more pucks and he steps into the net.

"Let's see how many you can put in when there's someone in goal," he says jokingly.

I accept the challenge.

Puck after puck is flying towards the goal and I'm completely exhausted.

After successfully venting my frustration, we sit down, and my best friend puts his arm on my shoulder.

"You'll be fine, brother."

I inhale and exhale with difficulty.

"I flunked another exam, man," I say dejectedly, shaking my head.

"It's not that bad," he tries to cheer me up.

"I just don't understand this shit. If it goes on like this, I'm going to fail at everything."

Chase looks at me seriously.

"Maybe a tutor could help you?"

"No one will take me seriously as captain anymore if I need a tutor. I can't risk my reputation, Chase, you know that" I retort, annoyed.

"It's a suggestion, bro. I'm trying to help..."

"I know, I'm sorry. It's just that this whole thing is getting on my nerves."

He rubs my shoulder to reassure me.

"It's not a weakness to seek help, Liam. Just think about it."

We sit in silence for a while, then the guys from the team arrive for training.

"You're early," exclaims a puzzled Tyler.

Coach Franklyn is also surprised that we're already here, but he gives us a nod before clapping his hands.

"Let's go, boys!"

We're all skating on the ice and suddenly, out of the corner of my eye, I see Emily near the bench.

Once again, her aura captivates me.

Today, she has gathered her blonde mane into a braid, which makes her face stand out even more. I raise my hand in greeting and she smiles.

Before my body acts up again, I turn away and concentrate on my training. Might as well keep my distance!

Once showered, I quickly head home to avoid any distractions.

Fuck, this can't go on much longer...

Before falling asleep, I think long and hard about my situation. Is Chase right? Do I need a damn tutor?

Frustrated, I run my hands over my face. No! Somehow, I'll manage.

5

Liam

I wake up highly motivated before my alarm goes off. I'm determined to improve my grades and not miss any more exams.

So off I go to the library. It's a well-known fact that you learn best there. At least, that's what a lot of people say.

I look for a table in the corner and unpack my documents and books.

Maybe it would help if I approached the question strategically? But I'm a bit overwhelmed by all the information on the table in front of me. How do I take it all in?

Doubt begins to gnaw at me and my determination from earlier is already crumbling. I take a deep breath and simply reach for one of the books. How hard can it be? What the hell...

I open a chapter of the *Business and Economics* textbook and start taking notes.

Suddenly, someone taps me on the shoulder. I'm so absorbed in what I'm doing that I jump.

Emily?

My heart beats even faster.

"Hi," I finally articulate.

"Are you studying for an exam?" she asks, after greeting

me in turn.

"Something like that, yeah..." I answer, unable to take my eyes off her face.

Her eyes attract me like a magnet.

"I won't bother you any longer..."

She gives me a wave and disappears down an alley. With her, my concentration of a few minutes ago is gone. I lean back in the chair and watch her choose a book before sitting down at one of the tables.

I try to look away and regain my attention. My pile of books seems to have suddenly grown. I stroke my three-day beard and go back to studying. This time, I stay focused and when I look up, Emily has already left. I let my gaze wander and the clock above the door tells me it's now time to go to class.

I have to admit I'm a bit proud of myself. It wasn't bad for a start. Motivated, I gather my things and set off.

If I can hang in there over the next few weeks, I'm sure my performance will improve!

Over the next few days, I try to assimilate the new routine: learning, studying, training, doing homework. Even on weekends, I don't go out, trying to prepare for the upcoming exams.

The longer I hold out, the more confident I become. But I can't shake the feeling that something is missing. All the learning and training leaves little room for friends and fun. Once again, I'm sitting in front of my homework when my cell phone rings.

"What's up, bro?" I say, picking up the phone.

"Dude, you're still alive? Except on the ice, we don't see you anymore!" exclaims Chase.

"I try to be a model student, you should try."

I'm afraid my point is lost.

"Come and have a beer with us," he invites me.

"Chase, I really need to study for this stupid exam," I retort.

At the same time, I hear a knock on my door. Phone in hand, I get up and open the door. Chase is standing in front of me, smiling.

"No discussion," he says, hanging up.

I roll my eyes.

"You can't study all the time, Liam, you need to have some fun too. Otherwise, your unaccustomed brain will overheat. Just a beer with your best mate…"

I sigh.

"Okay, okay, give me a minute, I'll get dressed," I finally relent.

A beer can't hurt me, after all…

"With all your studying, now, did you get to see the famous reporter again?" asks Chase as we sit in the campus sports bar.

I raise an eyebrow.

"No… And why would I want to see her again?"

"Don't tell me you're not indifferent to her, because there's more than one of us on the team who've noticed her hellish ass."

Oddly enough, this remark ruffles my hair and I feel very upset. Where are they ogling Emily from?

"We get along well, that's all, and when we see each other, it's only for the articles she has to write. Do you really have nothing else to do but watch everything that goes by, my word!"

"Oh, fine! As if you hadn't noticed!" exclaims Chase, laughing.

"Is that why you dragged me over here, to tell me about her?"

I don't like the way this conversation is going; let alone how I feel when Chase tells me they've all got it in for her. These guys are dogs!

Because you're not one? The guy starts studying after years of laziness, and suddenly he's better than the others...

"Don't take it like that, Liam. You know you can tell me anything, don't you?" advances Chase in an uncertain voice.

Damn it! Why don't I even confide in my best friend? But at the same time, I have such a hard time admitting to myself that I like this girl, so why should I tell my buddy?

"I find her a little interesting, yeah... But it doesn't make any sense! I've got to concentrate on the season. The team's counting on me. And I've got to get better grades too. Coach Franklyn has me in his sights, and he's right, I need to be able to secure a future on all fronts, like a big guy. Hell, I can do it!"

Chase nods.

"I understand, but I don't think anyone will hold it against you if you treat yourself to a little happiness..."

"Thanks, man. But can we change the subject, please? I can't do this right now, anyway. I've got to get my life in order first. I've finally got a rhythm going, and I can't let it go."

Chase smiles and takes a sip of beer.

"No problem, Romeo. Anyway, I've already forgotten what we were talking about..."

I laugh and down the rest of my beer.

We keep joking for a while, which feels really good. Chase always knows how to take my mind off things. I even feel slightly drunk and all my worries seem forgotten.

I let my gaze wander around the bar and stop on a pair of eyes looking at me with interest. This attractive woman is sending me clear signals. I probably shouldn't say no to this welcome distraction. Yet something is different from usual. My body simply doesn't move; it sits as if glued together. Even my dick doesn't give off any vibrations, and that's very unusual! That's when Emily's laughter bursts into my mind. I shake my head to get rid of it and concentrate on my best friend.

He raises his beer to toast, imitating the coach. I can't stop laughing. If it wasn't for Chase, I couldn't stand it.

When he takes his leave and stumbles on his way out, I laugh again. I feel free and relaxed. And for the first time in weeks, I fall asleep with a smile on my face.

★★★

My stomach contracts as the teacher hands out a test without warning, and I sigh. Slightly hungover and tired, I'm not in the best of moods. But I do my best.

In the end, I think all this learning has served a purpose and I feel I've answered pretty well.

But the next day, when we get the test results, I can hardly believe it.

Another fucking failure.

Angrily, I leave the lecture hall and rush through the university corridors so fast that I hit someone.

Emily... *What the hell kind of cosmic joke is this?*

"Watch where you're going," I growl and get ready to leave again.

"Are you all right, Liam?" she asks behind my back.

The concern in her voice makes me stop.

"No. Nothing's going right, if you ask me," I let out in a breath.

"Ho... You want to talk about it?"

"Not really."

She seems to think for a moment, her cheeks turning pink, as if her future boldness is costing her.

"Let me take you out for coffee," she offers gently, making me feel guilty for having spoken badly to her.

I run my hand through my curly hair. Fuck... If that isn't raw temptation! I can't help accepting her invitation. In her presence, my shoulders feel lighter.

We enter the café where Chase works and sit down at a corner table. Emily orders us a coffee. For a moment, we sit in silence. My eyes are fixed on my cup, and I know I have to say something.

"Thank you, Emily. I think that's what I needed to keep from hitting a wall..."

I look up at her and smile to lighten the mood. Her body suddenly relaxes, and she in turn gives me a warm, sincere smile.

"What's got you in such a state?" she asks bravely, given the contradictory signals I keep sending her.

"It's complicated... I've failed several tests and exams this semester. If this keeps up, I'm not going to graduate. No matter how hard I study, I just don't understand this shit."

Her mouth opens slightly in surprise.

"Yeah, you can laugh. Liam Scott wants to graduate! Now that would be a big scoop for your paper!"

"I think it's admirable that you put so much effort into combining sport, which already takes up so much of your time, with your studies. Many athletes are content with their results in the discipline they practice. Why do you want to get your diploma?" she says shyly.

I sigh and look at her frankly.

"Hockey is my life. It's all I've ever had. It's my world, and hopefully my future. But... do we really know what tomorrow will bring? I'm not a moron. The coach called me to order. I'll have an even better record in the eyes of recruiters if I have a good hockey season, as well as good grades. Then, I might as well take advantage of my time at university to go out with something in my pocket. I mean something more than a professional league contract."

I stretch out a smile.

I'm amazed at how easy it is to talk to her. Putting my current problems into words not only relieves me, but also helps me to see things more clearly, to regain my confidence and motivation. That, and the bright look she's giving me right now.

Damn, she's beautiful...

She's not disappointed, not mocking. No, she's attentive and seems concerned by what I'm telling her. My heart skips a beat when I realize that I like this girl. Yeah, I really like her, actually. Crazy...

"I... I can help you if you want," she says. "We can study together, if you like. I think it's easier for two people. Even if... If our subjects are different, eh..."

She blushes immediately after formulating her proposal. I'm standing there like an idiot, staring at her in astonishment. My first instinct is to refuse her offer and get out of there as fast as my feet will carry me, but her eyes hold me prisoner. I can't move. And I don't want to.

It's time I swallow my pride too.

Then you'd spend more time with her, smart-ass!

I silence my subconscious and nod.

"It's really nice of you to offer. Really... Your help would be invaluable, because right now I don't know where to start with my lessons."

My anger from earlier evaporates instantly and I feel a gentle warmth burning in the pit of my stomach.

Come on, man, it's only for your studies! Cool it !

6

Emily

I just offered Liam Scott my help. Me. Emily Hansen. I've just dared to offer my help to the captain of the university hockey team, the campus hottie, and incidentally the notorious womanizer that he is. I've just thrown myself into the lion's den. But I think I'm enjoying the fangs...

I swallow when he accepts. I can hardly believe my ears.

He agreed!

I avert my eyes from his gaze, which seems to probe and read my innermost being, before clearing my throat. I try to ignore the horde of butterflies raging in my stomach.

"Great!" I exclaim, my voice almost hoarse.

"How do you want to proceed?"

"The best thing would be to exchange numbers so that we can set up a meeting... I mean, a date to study something..."

I'm still blushing. *Silly girl.*

Liam nods slowly. Asking for help probably isn't one of his strong points. I can tell by the look on his face when my proposal becomes more concrete.

Nevertheless, he hands me his cell phone and I type in my number.

"If you're worried about it, we can keep it between us. I

won't tell anyone, I promise."

"Thanks, Emily. It's not that I want to make a secret of it, but yeah, with my captain status... Um... It would be awkward if anyone finds out I need a hand," he replies when I hand him back his phone.

Especially coming from the first year I am, not necessarily popular and not necessarily cool. I get it!

Liam stands up and scratches his chin.

"Well, I'll... I'll see you around... And thanks for the coffee. I'll..."

He hesitates.

"I'll see you soon!" he says simply, before running off in a huff.

This guy is weird... Is it too much shame for him to be seen with me for more than an hour? Then, you can't ignore the fact that he's already flirted with me, and it's as if at the same time he's trying to get away from me or that I'm annoying him, and so he ignores me. I think I was too nice when I offered to help him.

I pout, disappointed.

As I watch him go, my doubts start to creep in. Have I just made a big mistake? I should be concentrating on my studies, not playing tutor. I've got so much more to do with the paper. Not to mention the fact that I'm studying something completely different. But Liam's doing the business management course, and as my dad's a pretty successful businessman, I know quite a bit about it...

I sigh.

Whatever happens, I mustn't lose my concentration if I want to succeed in getting into a big newspaper. I need to set some rules before studying with him, so it can really stay within a serious and useful framework for both of us. Yes, that sounds good!

On the way home, I'm thinking about the best way to organize things.

In any case, the most important point is that I have to control my reactions. Liam is incredibly seductive, and he knows it. I don't know what his game is with me, blowing hot and cold, but I mustn't let myself be fooled. Girls like me don't get with guys like him, and vice versa. We can't let ourselves get distracted. And he told me in an interview: for him, sport comes first.

***

I'm sitting in my media management class, diligently taking notes. The subject isn't as difficult as I first thought. I've managed to retain the most important points and understand the broad outlines. That's pretty positive!

For the umpteenth time, I glance at my phone. I hate myself for doing this, but I still haven't heard from Liam, and I can't help feeling disappointed. He's probably changed his mind about us working together... I can't force him! It's up to him.

I will probably see him soon anyway, as today I'm off to hockey practice. I have to cover the team's preparations for the newspaper, as there's another big game this weekend. Coach Franklyn is still hoping that my articles will attract the attention of sports agents.

In any case, readers seem to enjoy my writing, and spectators are always more numerous at each game. Maddie and my editor are also very satisfied with my work so far. I'm very motivated by this confirmation. It feels good to know that I'm on the right track.

Arriving at the rink, I take my usual seat on the substitutes' bench. Before the boys come out of the locker room, I still have ten minutes to spare. I take a few notes that will help me structure my future article. Finally, I hear them arrive. I notice that Liam looks tired and I feel guilty for thinking that, if he hadn't contacted me, it was out of lack of consideration. I suppose he has a busy life too. And with the game coming up, he must surely be training hard.

When he passes me on the ice, he barely nods. This little game of pretending I don't really exist is starting to get on my nerves!

I lose myself in my thoughts, and it's a whistle from the coach that brings me back to reality.

Crap.

Liam is becoming too much of a distraction. Instead of observing the training and analyzing what's going on, I'm busy thinking about him.

I shake my head, concentrate on my notebook and write down a few impressions.

Today, the captain is slower than usual. It's in stark contrast to his usual fiery spirit, which seems to have repercussions for the rest of the team. Everyone lacks the drive and bite that normally characterize them. It's interesting to observe how much the atmosphere on the ice depends on the captain. I can understand the pressure on Liam.

Passes have no impact, the puck gets lost, sticks bang and bang. It feels like they're in slow motion, and if I can see it, so can Coach Franklyn, who's getting tenser by the minute.

"Holy shit! What the hell is this? Liam, move! Eliot, tighten up on your skates, for God's sake! Chase, do you want me to get you a coffee, maybe? What's the matter with you today?" finally yells the latter.

He kicks the fence surrounding the rink and continues to scream at the whole team. The name calling continues and I shrink back to my bench. Suddenly, as if remembering that

I'm there, he turns to me. His index finger points at me, and I feel an aura of anger emanating from him.

"And you, not a single word about this in your notebook! If you write anything about this catastrophe, believe me, you'll be in trouble!"

I swallow nod and quickly gather my things. I'd rather not witness this disaster any longer and stay on the coach's radar.

Once in my student room, sitting on the sofa, I sigh. That was just awful! I reread my notes, but no positive words seem to fit such a horrible training. I want to be nice, but there are limits. The coach is right, I might as well not write anything down... Too bad! I'll concentrate on the game.

Suddenly, my phone vibrates, announcing the arrival of a message. The number is unknown and I unlock the screen with a frown.

* *Hello Emily. This is Liam. Can we see each other tomorrow at noon to study?*

This guy's got some nerve! I roll my eyes and toss my phone aside in frustration. If he thinks I'm going to answer him right away, as soon as he writes me a poor text message when he barely said hello earlier, he's mistaken. After days of radio silence, he deserves to stew a bit!

I open my laptop and choose a film. Immersing myself in another world for a while will do me good.

After half an hour, I'm already feeling calmer. I finally grab my smartphone and type a reply to the damn captain.

* *All right. At the library, at noon tomorrow.*

There you go. I didn't say 'hello' or 'are you all right?' I remained firm. Proud of myself, I put the phone down before it vibrates again for an answer.

* *Thank you*

Well, I don't know what to expect tomorrow, but deep down I feel a restlessness, which makes me think that I'm not insensitive to the idea of studying with Liam Scott.

The library doors close behind me as I spot Liam sitting at one of the tables, his eyes riveted to his notes. He seems lost in thought as I approach.
"Hi," I say, sitting down next to him.
An annoyed "shh" comes from a corner of the room and I put my hand in front of my mouth. Oops...
Liam raises tired eyes to me, and he gives me a weak smile.
"Hi," he replies in a low voice, rubbing his chin.
He really looks like he's at the end of his rope, and I feel guilty that I thought he was snubbing me. Obviously, it's something else, and he seems to be struggling with a whole host of problems.
"You don't look so good..." I say timidly.
"I really have a lot of catching up to do if I'm going to pass the next exam. With the game coming up, it's hard for me to keep up with everything. That's why..."
He seems to hesitate for a moment, as if embarrassed.
"That's why I decided to send you a message," he continues. "I'm not in the habit of asking for help, but right now I'm struggling."
His confession touches me and I nod.
"All right, then. Where do you want to start? What's your study methodology?"
He opens his round eyes and stares at me, as if I've just said something atrocious, or spoken a foreign language.

"I... Uh... My methodology..."

He pushes a notebook full of shapeless notes, scribbles and numbers towards me.

"Oh, yeah. Well... I think we're going to go over the basics a bit so you can get better organized. Sound good?"

I smile at him to lighten the mood, and he gives me a sincere smile that warms me from head to toe.

Damn, he's handsome!

"That's fine by me! And... thank you, Emily. I really..."

I sweep away his thanks with a wave of my hand as if it's no big deal, and we both lean back over his notebooks, our heads strangely close together. I feel his spicy scent returning to my nostrils and the butterflies in my stomach awaken.

No, no... Not now! Concentrate!

I end up dissecting his working method. He recognizes that I'm more organized, which makes me laugh. Through my university studies, I've learned by default to be structured in everything I do: an article has a starting point, a statement, a thread and a conclusion. I use all these points in my everyday life. Liam seems to like the way I do things, and we make a few lesson plans together. He's a quick learner and a studious one. He asks the right questions, takes notes and makes a real effort. I like that about him.

He rubs his three-day beard, his brown curls falling over his forehead.

"That's much better! It's crazy!" he exclaims softly, so as not to disturb the other students.

"You're doing a really good job," I remark.

"Your help makes all the difference! I'm such an idiot for not contacting you sooner!"

The joy in his eyes warms my heart. It's good to know I can help him. Whatever happened with him during the last training session, or during our last meetings, seems to have evaporated. Nor are there any misunderstandings, flirtations or long, icy silences. How nice! I feel like I'm discovering him in his true light, and I like that.

Calm down, Emily!

As we pack up, Liam asks:

"Tomorrow, how about we meet at the same time? Are you free?"

I look at him, hiding my surprise, and smile.

"Yes, no problem."

"Are you sure about this? It doesn't slow you down in your own work, does it?"

"No, don't worry. You'll settle in gradually, and I'll be able to study my subjects and you yours, without it slowing us down."

He smiles broadly, as if relieved.

"Great!"

As we say goodbye, he seems to hesitate, he raises his arm, motions towards me, and finally taps me on the shoulder as if I were one of his buddies. Disappointment twists my heart, and I try to pull myself together to put on an appropriate smile.

No, but seriously? Liam Scott wasn't going to hug me for studying for over an hour together, was he? What an idiot I am...

"Goodbye, Liam," I mumble, turning on my heels.

Lost in my thoughts, I take the wrong route back to my room and wander around the campus for a while. After a while, I pull myself together and get back on the right road. I hope Cassy isn't back yet. She might see that something's bothering me, and I can't see myself admitting to her that I've got a thing for the university playboy. It's hard enough for me to understand what's going on!

The next day, we meet at the library, and end up agreeing

on a daily meeting.

Our study sessions go on in the same studious way as the first. But I notice that every day I'm looking forward to spending more time with him.

It's not just about learning together. We laugh about our mistakes, discuss our opinions on certain subjects and share our thoughts on the world we live in. Little by little, I get the impression that a bond is forming between us that goes beyond simply sitting next to each other and dissecting our lessons.

I'm discovering a more mature person than I thought, more inclined to have interesting opinions on things other than sport, and above all with a sense of humor. Of course, he's terribly sexy. But let's just say that's not his main character trait in the end. That's for sure!

Today, we've completed a good work session, and Liam stares at me for a few seconds, seemingly searching for his words. I pretend not to have noticed and keep my eyes glued to my media rights manual, unable to read a single line.

"Emily?" he finally says softly.

"Hm?" I answer, looking at him as stoically as possible.

My heart is pounding in my chest, and I can't calm it down. All it takes is for his blue eyes to land on me insistently and my world shatters. This uncontrollable reaction both annoys and terrifies me. I know that one day our sessions will come to an end, and I'll go back to being the simple little journalist who writes articles about him and his team. The one who might have helped him get a good grade in an exam. I don't know what else I could be to a guy like him.

"Thank you," he continues. "Not only for your help, but also for our discussions. I feel like you understand me..."

Stunned, I feel my mouth round and close again. His words touch me. *Too much.*

"You don't need to thank me. I'm happy to help you and

also to have someone to talk to."

I try to give him a sincere smile. It's not that I don't want to, but right now I've got an irresistible urge to press myself against him, run my hand through his hair and do things to him that you wouldn't normally do in a library - well, normally, because I'm pretty sure Maddie's already had sex here!

I swallow at having such naughty thoughts and tense up that he might eventually read me. It doesn't seem to fail, because his smile widens, and his eyes start to sparkle.

Shit... You'd think I was talking out loud from the look on his face.

It both distresses and comforts me. Does he like me, even a little? A tenth of the appreciation I have for him would be a lot!

"Good luck on your exam tomorrow!" I finally blurt out to ease the tension.

For a brief moment, a shadow passes before his eyes.

"Thank you," he mutters.

I gather my things and get up.

"Keep me posted! See you at Saturday's game."

"Yes... See you later," mumbles Liam.

I turn on my heels and almost run away.

★★★

I'm having trouble concentrating on my course. I'm thinking about Liam and his exam. I really hope our study sessions have paid off!

Subconsciously, I check my cell phone every few minutes, hoping that he'll send me a message when he's finished. Yet the day goes by without a word. I'm really disappointed and find it hard to put on a brave face. It's crazy that this guy can have such an impact on me! I curse myself for reacting this way, but I can't stop my thoughts and my heart from going in all directions.

Finally, in the evening, I decide to send him a message. I've got to know for sure! Then again, it's also a way of getting back in touch...

* *Hi Liam, how did your exam go?*

I see that he's writing a reply and I wait, but nothing comes. I sigh and am about to let go of my phone when a message appears.

* *Not bad at all*

No punctuation. Not even an exclamation mark. Nothing. 'Not bad at all.' He could at least have written, 'Hi'. I don't know what I was expecting, but I feel annoyed by this response.

My phone vibrates again and my heart misses a beat, but it's a message from Maddie. She's suggesting we go to a party at one of her friends' houses tonight. Cassy will meet us there.

A girls' night out sounds like a good idea to get Liam out of my head. I tell her I'm up for it and immediately start getting ready.

Thirty minutes later, there's a knock on the door. Half-dressed, I jump up to open the door for Maddie.

She hugs me, euphoric.

"Why aren't you ready yet?" she asks, examining me from head to toe.

I groan.

"Give me five more minutes!"

I have a hard time deciding on my outfit, and finally pull out a low-cut top from my wardrobe. I slip on some heeled ankle boots and turn to my best friend. Maddie looks at me and whistles approvingly.

"Too low-cut?" I ask, unsure.

"No! It's perfect, sweetie. You're sexy!"

Arm in arm, we set off. When we get there, we enter the fraternity house hosting tonight's party, when Cassy comes running up to us, shouting joyfully and hugging us.

"I'm so happy to see you! Cute outfit, Emily!"

She looks me up and down with appreciation and I can't help but laugh.

The whole house is surprisingly full, and I notice that the hockey team seems to be there too. I pout and scan the crowd until my eyes meet those of Liam. His gaze settles on me for a moment, then he gives me a charming smile and winks. I answer soberly, nodding. Yet I can't stop a treacherous warmth spreading through me and end up looking away so that my flushed face doesn't reflect my emotions.

"I have to go to the bathroom," I announce to my friends.

"What, already?" exclaims Maddie.

"I'll see you later."

I get out of the way so as not to remain in the seductive captain's line of sight. I still feel his eyes on me, and I continue to liquefy by the minute.

It's got to stop!

No sooner have I firmed up on this idea than I brush past someone as I make my way into the crowded main room. I look up and catch Liam's azure gaze, which electrifies me even more at such close quarters. My body throws lightning bolts where we touched, and I continue to charge ahead before he calls out to me.

Alone at last, with the toilet door closed behind me, I take a deep breath. I lean over the sink and cool my rosy cheeks with cold water.

This is nothing. All this is nothing. I can have a good time with my friends. His presence won't change the course of my evening.

After a few deep breaths, I've calmed down a bit and feel ready to go out again.

When I open the door, Liam is standing right in front of it. His eyebrows are furrowed, and he seems to be deep in thought. Finally, he looks up and scrutinizes me.

"Hi Emily," he says.

With his fingertips, he sweeps a brown lock from his forehead and approaches me gently as I back away, ending up against the door at my back. His gaze roams over my face, and his tongue licks his lips.

What's he looking at? Has the water ruined my make-up?

Slowly, he places his left hand beside me, blocking my access to the corridor, and soon does the same with his right arm.

There's no way out.

My heart is racing. We've never been this close on purpose. I don't understand what he's playing at. Or at least, I'm afraid I do. I feel my whole body tense up, and the hollows of my thighs heat up.

He then leans towards me and stops just inches from my face. I swallow, my eyes still locked on his. I mustn't give in; I mustn't let him do this to me.

But I want him so much...

Just as I'm about to give up, he lowers his head, right next to my lips. His breath exudes a faint scent of alcohol and fruit. His scent envelops me. His warmth overwhelms me. I feel the pressure of his firm torso against my chest and my lower abdomen stirs.

"You look damn sexy tonight, Emily," he whispers.

Shivers run down my spine, threatening to bring me to my knees. I'm incredibly hot. This guy is the devil himself. But a very attractive devil!

Before I can say anything, a voice calls out to him from the other end of the corridor.

"Liam? Where are you, buddy?"

He winks at me before stepping back. He walks quietly up the corridor and disappears into the crowd. I stand there, petrified.

What the hell was that?

We were supposed to have a professional relationship! Well, yeah, I was hoping for more... I can't deny it. But now... we've made a big leap! He's trying to seduce me openly! Was he drunk? Maybe even high? No, I don't think so. The coach would smash his head in and he's too keen on his sporting career. It was just mind-blowing!

Now, even a deep breath or cold water on my face wouldn't be enough to calm me down. My legs won't obey me, and I can't think straight. I lean my head against the door and wait for my body to recover.

"Ha, there you are!" exclaims Maddie as she approaches me. "How are you? You look funny."

"Uh, yes... I have a headache, but it'll pass," I lie.

Maddie gives me a scrutinizing look and finally nods.

I feel guilty about lying to my best friend, but I don't feel ready to tell her everything right now.

Together, we hurry to the bar. She orders me a large glass of water and takes an aspirin from her purse.

I accept both gratefully and drink the cold water greedily. It helps to refresh me a little and get me back on my feet.

At the other end of the bar, Liam, surrounded by his teammates, glances at me with a satisfied smile. I ignore him and focus on my friends. Cassy and Maddie are chatting happily, and I pretend to listen. In spite of myself, my gaze regularly wanders to Liam and each time, our eyes meet. The more time passes, the more restless I become.

"Earth to Emily," says Cassy, patting me on the shoulder.

"Huh?" I reply.

She laughs.

"Are you listening to us?"

"Sorry... I think I'd better go home; my headache won't go away."

They look disappointed, but say nothing. I decline their offer of a lift and hug them in turn before leaving.

The fresh air does me a world of good.

As I walk back to my university building, the scene from earlier is replayed in my head.

How can I study with Liam now? That's all right, he can manage on his own now. But what about the interviews I have to do at every game? How can I be relaxed in front of him after what's just happened?

★★★

On the day of the hockey team's game, I arrive at the rink just in time. The guys are still warming up on the ice and, predictably, the stands are overflowing with spectators. Coach Franklyn greets me, quick to apologize for the last practice where he yelled at me.

I take a seat on the bench and get out my camera to illustrate my article. As I focus the lens on Liam, he winks at me. Immediately, what happened at the party the other night comes to mind. No wonder women fall at his feet! He has an incredible charm... Embarrassed and confused, I put my equipment down beside me and take out my notebook.

The game begins.

The team seems to have regained confidence compared to the training session I attended the other day, and I put that down to the admonishments the coach must have given them.

Liam is excellent. This time, all his shots are on target. The crowd goes wild when the whistle blows for the victory of our university team. Another one! Even I get caught up in the infectious good mood and clap my hands. The players celebrate their success, and I take the opportunity to snap a few photos.

Before leaving, I ask Coach Franklyn a few questions. This way, I don't have to meet Liam in person. I find this tactic very clever, and I'm glad I thought of it.

I quickly pack up my things and head home to work, before the captain - who's too sexy - comes to meet me.

As I sit down at home and start writing my article, the vibration of my cell phone pulls me out of my concentration. It's Liam...

* *I thought we had to debrief together at the end of every game. What a disappointment to have learned that you had asked your questions to the coach... If you're ever in the mood come party with us.*

Reading his message, I feel angry, but also terribly attracted by the idea of joining him. My body reacts immediately, and it takes a lot of effort to suppress the urge to see Liam again.

This guy's got a lot of nerve!

* *I can't tonight, I'm busy*

A clear and concise message. I'm so proud of myself!
Another vibration immediately follows.

* *Come on, Emi, just for an hour!*

He insists... Does he really want to see me? Is this another game of seduction? Why is he trying to seduce me in the first place? I hope he hasn't made a bet with his buddies...

I think back to our encounters in the library, to this Liam who's so different, and I know he's hiding behind that air of a playboy who can have it all. If only he had enough self-confidence to be like that all the time. But anyway, I think I like every side of him! I'm so screwed!

I sigh. I can't deny it's nice to be wooed by such an incredibly attractive guy. Well... I can write my article tomorrow, can't I?

* *OK but just for an hour. Where are you?*

The pizzeria where I meet him is next to the campus. It's packed and the noise inside is insane.

Why did I give in?

Suddenly, I feel a warm presence on my back and a breath on the back of my neck that I'd recognize between a thousand and one. There's only one that has such an effect on my body.

"Good to see you," Liam whispers in my ear.

He turns me towards him and scrutinizes me with his shining eyes. A horde of butterflies dance in my stomach and my heart beats wildly. Liam's hands are still on either side of my shoulders and he's grinning with a smile that borders on indecency. I get the impression he's enjoying torturing me.

I swallow the lump in my throat and stammer out a less than charming 'hello'.

"Are you hungry?" he asks, letting go of me.

My shoulders tingle where his hands used to be.

"Uh, yes..." I struggle to articulate.

Liam disappears for a moment and returns with a plate containing various slices of pizza. As he hands it to me, my fingers brush against his and a bolt of lightning shoots through me, nearly knocking everything to the ground.

"Did you enjoy the game?" he asks nonchalantly, his gaze shifting from my lips to my eyes.

It looks like he's trying to make conversation, when that's the last thing he wants to do.

I nod without saying a word.

"Come and sit down."

As I look around for an empty seat, I suddenly feel Liam's hand on the small of my back. He pushes me through the crowd to a small table in the corner. I put the plate in front of me and sit down on the bench. To my surprise, Liam sits next to me, not opposite. Our legs touch lightly and my cheeks flush.

To keep my hands busy, I take a slice of pizza.

"You were really good today," I end by saying to fill the silence.

He laughs.

"Better than the training session you attended, yeah, for sure..."

"I didn't want to say it."

"Oh, you can. That day, I was really out of shape."

He scratches the back of his neck, as if this admission were costing him.

"I had a lot of things on my mind, including my difficulties in studying. And... your help really helped me see things more clearly."

He suddenly looks up at me and I feel suspended in an abyss. I swallow my mouthful with some difficulty. His arm slips behind me on the back of the seat, like it's natural, and his body turns slightly towards mine. We look into each other's eyes again.

The tumult around us echoes in my ears like absorbent cotton. I can think of nothing but the desire to feel his lips on mine.

"Isn't the pizza good?" he asks mischievously.

I look away and bite hastily into my margarita, while he grabs a piece to do the same.

He's doing it on purpose, I'm sure. He's playing with my nerves!

It's confusing, but now that we're sitting side by side and just eating, I feel good and my body relaxes. We can be together in silence, without it feeling weird.

When we've both finished, Liam smiles in satisfaction and leans in a little closer to me. He looks deep into my eyes, and I feel as if I'm drowning in the ocean of his blue irises.

"I really have to keep working on my article," I exclaim suddenly.

"Let me take you home," he offers.

"Don't you want to take advantage of your evening to celebrate your victory?"

"No, I have to study again tomorrow. Now that I've got a good teacher, I mustn't waste these efforts," he replies with a casual smile.

I look at him thoughtfully for a moment, then finally nod, as if guided by a remote control.

As we stand up, he puts his hand on the small of my back again and we maneuver through the crowd.

We barely speak the whole way. To tell the truth, it's only a ten-minute walk and I feel like I'm walking on cloud nine.

Once we're in front of my residence, I rummage in my purse for my key.

"Thank you and good night, Liam," I say before turning towards the door, leaving him little choice as to the outcome of this evening.

"Good night, Emily."

The sound of my name in his mouth electrifies me, and I try to put the key in the lock so as not to snap. But behind my back, I don't hear his footsteps receding, on the contrary, he's drawing closer to me and once again the warmth of his presence stuns me.

That's when my body takes control of my mind. I turn around and find myself very close to him. Unable to resist, I grab his jacket and close the distance between us. Rising on tiptoe, I search for his lips.

7

Liam

Her lips are on mine. And she made the first move. I can hardly believe it.

My heart is racing, and I feel like I've been struck by lightning. I'd been dreaming of this moment for so long, and now it's as if I've been transported. A tingling runs through my body, followed by an incredible shiver. Her kiss tastes of honey, of temptation, and also of something more... Is this what Eve felt when she bit into the apple in the Garden of Eden?

Now's the time to have a thought like that!

As my hands press her against me, our tongues meet, our embrace becomes more intense, all of a sudden, an icy coldness grips my face. Emily has stepped back. Her fingers are no longer clinging to me, and it's as if I've just been violently deprived of something. Something good. Extremely good.

"Good night, Liam," she murmurs before unlocking the damned door and disappearing into her dorm.

For a few minutes, I stand there, perplexed. A thunderous erection twisting my dick in my too-tight jeans. Then I realize the obvious: she's gone, and left me there like a dying beast.

On the way back to the pizzeria, I can't help but turn the situation on its head. And paradoxically, I smile like an idiot.

One of those goofy smiles that have always made me hate people in love.

In love? Wow, calm down, man!

However, I am aware that what just happened was a mistake. A huge mistake. A mistake I've been wanting to make for some time now. This girl has been on my mind for weeks. During our study sessions, I completely melted. Shoehorned, trapped, caught in the grip of her blue eyes, and she was oblivious.

Is that what I like about her? That she doesn't realize the undeniable charm she has?

Truth be told, I love everything about Emily. When she nibbles her pen, when she tucks a blonde lock behind her ear, her concentration, her bursts of good humor, her passion for journalism, and her ass too. Because yeah, she really is gorgeous.

I sigh.

I'm in deep shit.

And despite that, I want more. The kiss we shared only fueled my desire for her. The fact that she's pushing me away only makes it worse.

Yeah, I'm playing with fire.

When we left for our last work session, I felt angry with her. She was implying that she had done her job, and that I was just a student to be coached. I felt like a jerk because I was already on my knees in front of her. That's why it took me so long to tell her that I'd more or less passed my exam. I wanted to see if she'd care. Her message made me jump to the four corners of my room, and for all that, I played the asshole by replying very succinctly. Seeing her then at this party, so sexy, so desirable, and at the very least disturbed by my presence, gave me a surge of hope. Driven by the alcohol and the festive atmosphere, I broke down and went to flirt with her. I had to know for sure. And I was right!

Icebound Attraction

From then on, I grew wings. And now that I've just taken off, I'm tumbling down. But for all that, I know it's dangerous to try to regain momentum. Very dangerous.

Is there room in my life for Emily Hansen? I swear by hockey...

When I return to our table, the guys are still talking about the game. I join them and don't let on. But I'm having trouble following their conversation. The kiss keeps popping into my mind.

A taste of honey, temptation and fear...

★★★

I'm sitting in the lecture hall, trying to concentrate on what the professor is saying.

Since Saturday night's kiss, I haven't spoken to Emily. I haven't run into her either. I wanted to write to her, but I don't know how to approach her. Then, should I really do it? Or rather, is it honest of me to keep hanging around her when I know a relationship isn't an option? I need to concentrate on my future. On hockey.

But... isn't it possible to reconcile everything?

Dude, you're already barely getting by with your classes and workouts, don't add a couple relationship to the picture!

I let out a long sigh and rest my head on the table.

I'm fucking fed up...

I finally decide to send her a text, one that leaves no room for refusal on her part. If I see her face-to-face at least one more time, maybe everything will clear up and I'll know what to do.

* *Hi Emily. I'll be at the library at noon waiting for you. See you later!*

Well done, Liam!

She doesn't reply, but I give it my best shot, and at the appointed hour, I'm there. As I unpack, I'm still lost in thought.

The short time I've spent with Emily so far has been unlike anything I've experienced before. I simply feel at ease with her, and her support helps to stabilize me. But a woman like Emily deserves someone who brings the world to her feet, and I'm just not in a position to do that right now. Ice hockey comes first.

As always, Emily is punctual. She seems a little nervous as she approaches me.

"Hi," she says shyly as she sits down at my table.

"Hi! Are you okay?" I ask, suddenly hesitant.

"Uh yes... Hum... What do you want to study today?"

She rummages through the books in front of her, seemingly out of the blue. Oh, she wants to play it that way? Pretend like nothing happened the other night? That's not going to make my job any easier, that's for sure!

We start studying. Every now and then, my arm brushes against hers, and I feel as if I'm getting little electric shocks. Her hands also shake a little as she turns the pages of her textbook. I watch her stealthily, wondering if I'll have the balls to talk to her.

After a while, I pluck up the courage to open my mouth. But nothing comes out. Absolutely nothing.

Okay. It's over.

The rest of the hour passes silently, and neither of us seems determined to broach the subject of our kiss. Eventually we say our goodbyes and I head off to lunch with the team, resigned.

Later, in the locker room at the ice rink, I can't get the little blonde out of my head. I've got to do something, damn it! So, I get my phone out of my bag and send her a message.

Are you free tonight? Can we get together after training?

I put down my phone and put on my skates. Just as I stand up, her reply arrives.

Yes. Where?

She's really good at keeping things short when she wants to! Is she giving me a run for my money?
I send her my address.
Knowing that I'll be talking to her later helps me focus on training and I feel more serene.
After sweating it out and giving it my all, I take a quick shower and rush home. I should clean up a bit before Emily arrives. Not that I am messy, but I'd still like to make a good impression on her.
That's a new one...
Despite myself, I'm feeling nervous, and at the stroke of 7p.m., I hear a knock on my door.
Suddenly, my heart is pounding and I open my hand, almost trembling.
"Thank you for coming."
"Please..."
"Come on in!"
I push myself off the frame and let her into my student room. Cautiously, she steps forward and looks around, as if expecting to see the entire hockey team tucked away in a corner.
"Can I offer you something to drink?"
Emily hesitates for a moment, then finally nods. I take two beers out of my small fridge, open them and hand her one. I invite her to sit on the couch and she continues to observe my world.

I feel a little intimidated having brought her into my personal space. Even though I've slept with a whole bunch of girls on campus, I always make sure they don't come to my room. It would be like inviting them into a part of my life, and I've always refused to do that. In the end, I was the one who suggested she comes. And so...

"Liam, why did you ask me to come?" she finally asks, staring at me with her big blue eyes.

I take a big sip and sit down next to her.

"I... er... so..."

The look on her face throws me off and I don't know where to start. And yet I've rehearsed my little speech dozens of times!

I put my beer on the table, and she imitates me, so that our hands bump into each other.

This simple contact triggers uncontrollable sensations inside me. My pants tighten, my reason stops, and I can't help but straighten up and press my mouth against hers.

Immediately, her lips receive me with the same surge of desire and my tongue savors hers. My hands grip her hips firmly, and I pull her onto me. She doesn't resist, and I feel her body pressing against mine, my crotch definitely on fire.

My fingers slide down her back, and I caress the curve of her butt. She moans against my mouth, supporting our kiss that hasn't stopped, and it's driving me crazy. Then I lift her shirt and explore her soft skin, reaching the clasp of her bra. She undulates her pelvis as if to urge me on, and I take that as consent. As I struggle with the fastening of her lingerie, her breasts press harder against my torso. Her hands clutch my hair and my mouth burns under her assault.

Damn, that's good.

I'm incredibly hot, my breathing is labored and my heart is almost out of my chest. I've never felt so attracted. Her lips make their way to my neck and she starts nibbling.

I moan in turn, and my hands follow the curve of her ribs to palpate her bouncing breasts. Under my palms, I feel her nipples harden, making my erection more painful. I need to see them, taste them, make them mine. This time, I break our contact to lift her top and toss it into a corner of my room. I remove her bra and release her magnificent breasts.

There, in front of me, topless, I admire her while she blushes a little.

"You're beautiful," I say.

She leans in to kiss me hungrily. I tip her onto the sofa with ease, sliding her into my arms. In turn, I straighten slightly to remove my T-shirt, starting a skin-to-skin that consumes me.

Emily moans softly under my procession of kisses. I lick her neck, her collarbone, and move slowly down to her breasts, which I suck greedily. They taste of spring and fruit. My tongue glides, rolls, plays with her nipples and I hear her voice getting hoarser and hoarser. Finally, I release her from my torture, to resume my journey towards her belly button, which I kiss my way through. My fingers are already working on the button of her jeans, which I open with ease. I catch a glimpse of her panties, which makes me hard as a rock. Any more and I'll be cumming like a prepubescent in my boxers...

I pull at her pants to rid her of them, exposing her shapely thighs in the process. Unable to bear it any longer, I press my mouth to her intimacy through the thin fabric of her purple lace, searching with my fingertips for an entrance. Above my head, a concert of pleasure rings out, and I feel all the more encouraged.

Gently, eager to make her tense up, I spread her panties to take greedy licks. As she squirms, my index finger enters her and I moan to feel her so wet. Her excitement seems to match mine, and I end up pulling off the last of her clothes, .

She doesn't complain, and lets me maneuver her thighs apart, slipping a hand into my hair, which she grabs with force. Here, I revel in her pleasure.

It's delicious. Really delicious.

Her moans increase as my tongue speeds up. I suck on her clit, my finger delving further, and suddenly she tenses, cries out, and I drink her in with relish.

The ambrosia of the gods.

Her orgasm is the most beautiful sound I've ever heard. With one hand, I unbutton my jeans and remove my boxers, freeing my dick which seems to leap out of its straitjacket. I sigh with pleasure, because I can't stand the cramped conditions any longer.

Straightening up on her elbows, Emily watches me, her tongue licking her lips greedily. She seems to enjoy what she sees and slides down on all fours on the sofa to take hold of me. With a firm hand, she jerks me off, sharing her flavor of a kiss with me. Then, slowly, with burning eyes, she descends between my legs to suck me off.

I hiccup as I feel her lips close over my dick and my mouth forms a circle as I exhale. I squeeze her bare butt as she thrusts me in and out against her tongue.

My hand grasps her hair, and I can't help but follow her movements, as in the most erotic dreams I've ever had about the two of us.

If she keeps this up, I'm gonna come...

Finally, she detaches herself from me, sucks on my glistening glans again and comes to sit astride my thighs. Her mouth nibbles my ear before whispering.

"Do you have a condom?"

I've got some! But I'm reluctant to tell her, as it wouldn't be the right moment. So, I reach over to the console behind the couch, pop the lid on a small basket, and grab a condom between two fingers. With a sure hand, I rip it off before slipping it over my more-than-stretched dick.

Emily then latches onto the back of my neck, and in a divine sensation, she comes to impale herself on me.

"Fuck..." I moan, as she begins to undulate her pelvis.

Not that I thought she was inexperienced, but her skill electrifies me. I give in and we soon find a common rhythm, surrendering completely to each other.

We're both close to climax and exchange kisses charged with desire, pleasure and lust. Her moans get louder and I can't hold back any longer. She makes circular movements with her hips, pushing us both towards orgasm.

Sweating and out of breath, she detaches herself from me and swings to my left, her head resting against my shoulder.

For quite a while, we stand there in silence, coming to our senses, and I wonder what could be going on in her head.

It wasn't planned. It really wasn't.

I was determined to distance myself, to tell her that we had to keep our relationship strictly 'professional' in the context of our studies and her job as a journalist.

You've done it, Liam!

I turn my head and look at her.

The sex with her was incredible. Emily is amazing!

Her eyes are closed, and she seems completely absent.

"Are you okay?" I ask, unable to stand the silence any longer.

"More than fine," she says, looking up at me.

"Would you like a drink?"

I stand up, grabbing my boxer shorts as I go before removing the condom. She nods and smiles.

"I think we can finish our beers..." she advances amused.

I run into the bathroom for a moment and when I come back, she's already dressed. I can't contain my disappointment at seeing her beautiful body back under her clothes.

She bites her lip, and I can see she wants to say something. Her gaze seems pensive and uncertainty suddenly shows in her eyes.

"Is something wrong?" I ask eyebrows furrowed.

"It was incredible, Liam..."

I smile broadly.

"I agree with you!"

"But..."

Sorry, what? A 'but'? Is she going to end up setting limits before I do? Or maybe she just didn't like it that much?

"This can't happen again," she finally says.

Surprised, I look at her, but say nothing, letting her continue.

"We both have very specific goals for our careers. And... we mustn't lose sight of them."

Wow!

I definitely misjudged Emily. It seems we have more in common than I thought. And yet, hearing it from her hurts. Maybe because she had the courage I lacked. I know she's right. I know it because it's what I want. But... I've become far more attached to her than I should be.

I look at the ground, shaking my head.

"I know what you mean. Our goals are important, and we can't let ourselves get distracted."

"Exactly. So, it's best if we remain 'friends', if that's okay with you."

She swallows, and I see her body tense up.

"It's possible, yes..." I finally concede.

"I don't want a relationship to jeopardize my studies. But at the same time, I don't want us to feel like we have to be apart either. I... I like you, Liam..."

A smile passes over my face.

"Good timing, I like you too!"
I look at her.
"Friends, then?" I conclude.
Emily thinks for a moment, then nods.

I feel both relieved and completely lost. I'm usually the one making this speech! And I really wanted to tell her. But paradoxically, it still gives me a hard time to consider being just friends with her.

A smile appears on Emily's face and I feel the tension between us ease.

"Thank you for your honesty, Liam," she says, sighing with relief.

"I should be thanking you."

I look into her eyes, then at her mouth and back again.

The agreement to remain friends seems to be the right decision. After this experience, it won't be easy, but it's better for both of us.

You try to convince yourself, that's good.

"It's good that we've put that aside. By the way, why did you ask me to come and see you tonight?" she asks, looking at me intently.

"Oh, I've... er... passed my exam and I wanted to celebrate with you," I stammer, forcing the corners of my mouth up.

"Liam! This is awesome!"

Excited, she claps her hands and hugs me. I hug her back and inhale her intoxicating scent, closing my eyes for a moment.

She gently pulls away from my embrace, and tugs at her shirt to straighten it.

"Well... I'd better be off, then," she says.

I walk her to the door, thank her and wish her a good night.

As I close behind her, I shake my head.

My god, what was that all about?

After a long shower, I finally go to bed. But sleep is out of the question. Her kisses, her lips, the feel of her fingertips on my skin, her passion, her orgasms - everything is etched in my memory. I can't get these images out of my head.

At the same time, I wonder why it was so easy for Emily to suggest that we stay friends, as if everything that had just happened was no big deal.

Have I done something wrong? She seemed satisfied. Or was she faking it? Maybe it wasn't what she'd expected? Or maybe that's it, it really wasn't much for her...

I rub my face with both hands.

Get a grip, Liam. This is exactly what you wanted in the end: no relationship, no temptations, no love.

8

Liam

The next day, we meet as usual at the library. Emily is already sitting at the table when I arrive and seems absorbed in something. When she sees me, she smiles warmly and waves. I sit down opposite her, keeping a certain distance between us. I can't trust myself in her presence.

While we're studying together, I get a bit distracted because I'm constantly careful not to touch her.

Emily also seems reserved.

It's probably the best way to go. The memories of our 'moment' are still fresh. With time, we'll certainly find a good balance, even if it seems complicated at the moment.

It's anything but easy! As soon as I'm near her, I get ideas. I banish them to the far corner of my brain and try to concentrate on the essentials, which proves rather difficult.

After our study session, we separate and return to our daily lives.

The next few days unfold in a similar way. We don't talk about the famous torrid evening, or anything personal. It's all about learning and supporting each other.

On the one hand, it's exactly what we both wanted, but on the other, I'd love nothing more than to hold her close to me again.

When I enter the lecture hall after our library session, everyone is talking about the new issue of the campus newspaper. I ask my seatmate if I can have a look. He hands me his copy, wide-eyed, and I find it hard to understand his attitude. Then I notice that on the front page, a photo of me takes up most of the space.

It's coming back to me. Emily had taken some photos last week. And when I winked at her, she captured the moment perfectly. I turn the pages to get to her article and am once again impressed by her talent as a journalist. Her choice of words and the emotions she generates are truly unique.

I return the newspaper to the guy I borrowed it from, and look down, trying to ignore the female students devouring me with their eyes.

The photo doesn't seem to please just me.

Shaking my head, I pull out my cell phone and text Emily before class starts.

* *Hi Em, great portrait, and fantastic article!*

I've attached three 'thumbs up' emojis that should be enough to express my enthusiasm.

At noon on the dot, I'm back at the library.

If I've learned anything from Emily, it's punctuality. As we enter the building, we almost collide and smile at each other. I wave her over and as she makes her way to our table, I can't help but admire her ass. So perfect and round.

Memories of the evening we spent together overwhelm me and warm me up a little too much.

Dude, calm down or you'll get an erection!

Breathing deeply, I try to sink back down before sitting down next to her.

"Shall we begin?" she asks, opening a book.

I stroke my jaw and nod. The sight of the curve of her loins seems to have distracted me more than anything, because I didn't hear her talking to me before that. Being just 'friends' isn't as simple as I thought. Not with her.

***

The hardness of the ice beneath my skates vibrates in my legs as I step onto the rink. The thud of the crowd in the background echoes in my ears. I tighten my helmet and let my gaze wander to the bench. When I see her, my heart starts to race.

The spotlights shine brightly on the ice, which shimmers with light blue and white. The energy and excitement of the spectators envelop me. I can clearly feel the adrenaline coursing through my veins.

Emily stands upright, her notebook with her - as always - next to Coach Franklyn. I give her a quick wave before taking up my starting position.

As kick-off sounds, my thoughts clear and I concentrate solely on the puck. My gaze meets that of the opposing captain, Lucas Stern, and I sense an electric tension between us. Lucas and I have been rivals for ages. Today's game isn't just a game, it's a competition for the favor of one of the sports agents sitting in the audience. Emily's articles have paid off and we've caught the eye of at least one of them.

And of course, the winner has a better chance of getting an interview.

My skates bite into the ice as I start moving and push the puck in front of me with my stick.

The spectators melt into a ghostly crowd as I concentrate on my teammates and try to pass the puck to them. But there's little room around me. I'm squeezed in close, and I try to thwart my opponents' attacks.

Suddenly, I see an opening and the puck slides at breakneck speed towards Chase. I free myself from my pursuers and my best friend steps towards me again, keeping hold of our most prized possession. My muscles tense as I accelerate towards the goal.

The keeper is ready, tense, knees bent, and Chase makes a decisive pass for me to shoot. Out of the corner of my eye, I see Emily press her hand to her mouth. I raise my stick and bring it down with force, feel the resistance of the puck and wait to see it get caught in the net.

Holy shit!

I've just missed it by inches! I don't usually miss this kind of shot and I feel anger twist my stomach. Chase looks at me quizzically, but I just shake my head and try to get back into the rhythm of the game. Passes fly, body charges follow, and we fight hard for every inch of ice. Every move is crucial.

The half-time whistle blows, and we return to the locker room without a point to show for it.

I take advantage of this break to regain my concentration and take stock. Emily broke my concentration. And I blame myself. It's not her fault, that's for sure. But it's obvious. If I hadn't glanced at her, I could have tapped on the window that was open to me.

I can't let that happen. Today's game is too important for me to let it go to waste.

Chase approaches me and pats me on the shoulder.

"Dude, don't let the agents pressure you. You're a great player. And, no shit, Liam, we can't let Lucas win!"

He laughs heartily and helps me to my feet.

"We'll make it, brother!" he insists.

I can feel myself relaxing a little.

Sweat breaks out on my forehead as I dive into the next

part of the game. Time seems to stand still as we battle on the ice - a mixture of brute force, skill and strategy.

As the end of the game approaches, I can feel the fatigue in my muscles. But it's the will to win that keeps me going. The crowd goes wild as I make my way to the goal again. It's just me and the net, and this time I ignore everything else. I shoot again, watch the puck slide across the ice and between the goalkeeper's legs.

A few seconds later, the final whistle blows, and I am intoxicated with joy and relief.

We won, admittedly by the skin of our teeth, but we won.

The cheers from the crowd and the hugs from my teammates around me warm my heart. The fact that we fought and won as a united team fills me with immense pride. Every second we spent together in training was worth it.

As we move away from the ice, I can't help thinking that ice hockey is more than just a sport. It's about teamwork, determination and fighting spirit. Every game is an opportunity to prove yourself and excel.

I take off my helmet and wipe the sweat from my forehead. I'd do anything for these moments, the exhilaration of victory and the prospect of a successful career.

Even give up on Emily?

Emily

The hum of music fills our room. Anticipation of the evening is in the air, as my friends and I prepare for an exciting night.

Maddie and Cassy chat happily to each other while they do my makeup. The energy in the room is infectious and I'm excited. Today there's a party on campus with live music - it's really a special night. And I've decided to leave my look entirely in the hands of Maddie and Cassy. They know a thing or two about styling, especially Cassy, and my roommate is totally into it. I wanted to think outside the box.

Maddie rummages through my clothes and Cassy's, looking for the perfect match. They agree behind my back, and hand me a pair of black skinny jeans, a red sequin crop top and rockin' black leather ankle boots. After a moment's thought, wondering if it's 'too much', I accept, determined to feel sexy.

"Emily, you look stunning," says Maddie, smiling at me in the mirror.

They clap their hands in satisfaction, happy with their work.

"Thank you so much! You look great too!"

Maddie wears a blouse with the first buttons undone and tight-fitting pants. Cassy opted for a short dress that she wears with boots.

When we finally set off, I feel a mixture of impatience and nervousness. Nights on campus have a special magic - it's a way of escaping everyday life in familiar surroundings and embarking on an exciting adventure.

Secretly, I hope this night will help me see my friendship with Liam as a 'real' friendship. Because so far, I'm having trouble controlling my feelings.

After our kiss, our hot evening and our agreement, I wanted to go and see him. I wanted to tell him that I wasn't sure I could consider this a simple friendship and that the whole thing made me uncomfortable. I wanted to open up to him about how I felt, to be honest, and above all to stop spinning it all around in my head, night after night.

So, I made my way to the locker room, where I knew I could find him, and I overheard a conversation... It was between him and Coach Franklyn. The coach was telling him that he shouldn't let himself get distracted, that the partying, the girls, and the mischief Liam was used to, could no longer be tolerated. That the games ahead were decisive for his career. I immediately turned around and went back to my room, my heart pounding.

That day, I vowed not to say a word about my true feelings. So, spending time with my friends is what I need.

On the way to the party, I can't help but smile. The bond with Maddie and Cassy is special - in good times and bad, we stick together and every minute we spend together is unique. They made my arrival at university so easy that I hardly had time to feel lonely and lost, and for that I'm infinitely grateful.

The lights set up around the campus twinkle and we walk towards the stage. The closer we get, the more the pulsating energy of the music envelops us. I feel more alive than I have in a long time as we immerse ourselves in the mass of people present. Colorful shadows glide over the crowd and the joyful atmosphere carries us along. I let the music guide me, moving my body to the beat and feeling free.

After a few songs, I signal to Maddie and Cassy that I need a drink. We weave in and out of the groups to reach the ephemeral bar set up in a corner of the campus. I slowly make my way to the counter, waiting for the people in front of me to be served, when I find myself standing next to an extremely attractive guy. He looks me up and down and makes no secret of his appreciation. Finally, he looks at my friends and smiles again.

"Can I buy you a drink?"

Determined to distance myself from my feelings for Liam, I nod in good humor. Maddie and Cassy look puzzled, but eventually nod in turn.

He orders for us and we stand to one side to collect our drinks.

"My name's Lucas, nice to meet you!" he says, handing us our glasses.

I point to my friends and myself in turn.

"This is Maddie, Cassy, and I'm Emily."

He gives me a more pronounced look, and after what seems like an eternity, he also turns to Maddie and Cassy.

"Are all three of you students here?"

"Yes! Aren't you?" I ask curiously.

"No, I'm just... passing through. I heard about this party, so I stayed a little longer."

He stretches out a charming smile.

"I'm not disappointed with the atmosphere on your campus..." he adds, continuing to devour me with his eyes.

"We don't have parties like this all the time but it's true that it's great," I chat, a little uncomfortable with his keen interest.

Maddie finishes her drink and gives me a sidelong glance. *Yeah, well, I get it, she's bored!*

"Would you like to come and dance with us?" I suggest, more out of politeness than any real desire.

"Yes!" replies Lucas, determined.

We make our way back into the crowd. Maddie and Cassy are so focused on each other that I have no choice but to dance with Lucas. We move together to the rhythm of the music and the more we dance, the more tension I feel between us. In the end, Lucas's closeness isn't so bad, and I end up relaxing. I've got to admit, he's pretty hot too!

"You look beautiful, Emily…" he throws at me between two lascivious movements, a rather explicit sparkle in his eyes.

My cheeks are getting hot.

"Thank you…" I stammer.

He moves closer to me, and one of his warm hands comes to rest on the small of my back. This somewhat daring contact doesn't bother me, and I let him. He leans closer and I feel his breath on my cheek.

"You and me - maybe we could go have some fun somewhere else, what do you say?"

His words shock me. Flirting, seduction, dancing and touching are all fine. But to suggest that we go off in a corner and have sex, no, I can't do it.

The dance floor seems to be shrinking and I feel the need to withdraw.

"I'm sorry, but I'm here to enjoy the evening with my friends," I reply, my voice firm.

He just laughs, a sound that gives me unpleasant chills.

"But you could also enjoy it with me."

My unease is growing. His advances are insistent, and I don't want to find myself in a situation I can't control. He's always glued to me, and I can't stand feeling that way.

"No, I'm fine where I am," I say, trying to free myself from his embrace.

But Lucas seems to tighten his grip. I hastily turn my head towards my friends and, seeing me do so, he reluctantly lets go. His gaze remains insistent.

"Give it some thought. I'm sure we could have a good time together."

I barely nod and finally move away from him to join Maddie and Cassy. The music and lights around me suddenly seem less exciting and I can't shake the idea of Lucas's advances.

My friends look at me with concern.

"How are you, beautiful?"

"I'm fine!"

I try to smile.

Now I'm out of danger. No need to sound the alarm. I glance over my shoulder to see if Lucas is still there, but he seems to have left. I try to concentrate on the dance, but my thoughts won't let me rest. Lucas' advances have thrown me off balance, and I feel uncomfortable and vulnerable. The evening that seemed so promising before suddenly seems less liberating.

"I'm going to sit down for a while."

"Oh, you want us to come with you?"

"No, no, enjoy! I'll be back in a minute!"

I need to get away, take a breath, regain my composure.

Tables and chairs have been set up not far from the ephemeral bar. The atmosphere is calmer, there are fewer people and the music is quieter. I sit down to take a short break. A glass of water will certainly do me good. I'm still slightly dizzy.

Suddenly, I feel someone sit down next to me. My heart quickens a little when I see that it's Lucas. A self-confident smile spreads across his face and he leans back against the table to look at me intently.

"Hey!" he says, his voice deeper than before.

I swallow.

"I saw you sitting there, all alone, and thought you might need some company. It's a pity that such a beautiful woman should be without someone at her side," he continues.

The memory of our previous conversation sends a chill down my spine.

"Lucas, I already told you I'm here to have fun with my friends."

He smiles insolently.

"Come on, you and I would have lots of fun, think about it. I'm sure deep down you're not that shy... Besides, I've spotted a great place where we could enjoy a moment together..."

At these words, I start to get angry.

"I think I've made it clear: I'm not interested!" I exclaim more loudly than I expected.

He then slides a hand over my knee, up my thigh. I freeze at his touch, tetanized.

"You should take no for an answer when a woman says no," suddenly growls a voice I know all too well from across the table.

Just as quickly, I feel myself lift off my seat and the next thing I know, Liam is between me and Lucas, like a shield.

"Oh, come on! Emily and I are having a friendly chat. Mind your own business, Captain Scott," retorts Lucas, annoyed.

"Does losing the game make you think you can act like a big jerk?"

"And the fact that you've won makes you grow wings, or rather balls?"

I sigh and turn to leave. I don't have the nerves for an argument between two alpha males!

As I walk away, screams ring out behind me, startling me. I turn around to find Lucas on the ground, his nose bleeding.

Oh boy...

"You're completely insane! You bastard!" exclaims the latter, a hand pressed to his face as he stands up.

Two security guards come running and narrowly prevent Liam from giving Lucas another blow.

I step back, dumbfounded.

What's gotten into him? This has gone too far!

Liam and Lucas are battling with security and continue to shout at each other like two rabid dogs.

Lucas Stern! What an idiot! He's the captain of the opposing team! The one that lost the hockey game.

I sigh.

While Liam defended my honor, he also settled scores with his opponents. And for what? Because they only won by one point? Because he missed a crucial goal?

I really don't get it. Am I really concerned by his sudden heroic and protective attitude?

It's definitely too much for me. I must leave.

As I make my way back to my room, my heart pounding, I send a message to Maddie and Cassy to let them know I am home. I say that my period has just come without warning and that I don't feel up to dancing anymore. Cassy replies that she'll probably spend the night at Maddie's so as not to disturb me if I'm asleep.

Once I'm alone, I turn over what's happened in every direction, struggling to sleep.

★★★

When I wake up, I'm still angry.

What possessed Liam to hit Lucas?

Without his intervention, I don't know how the whole thing would have ended. But all he had to do was stop the moment he pulled me to safety. There was no point in breaking his nose...

I look at my phone to check the time and see two missed calls and a message from him.

* *Em, how are you? Can we talk?*

I wrinkle my nose. It's absolutely too early for this, so I duck back under my blanket.

After a few minutes of staring frustratedly ahead, I hear the key in the door and Maddie and Cassy's voices. I sigh silently and extricate myself from the blanket that envelops me like a second skin.

When they see me, they greet me in chorus.

"Hi there!"

"Hi," I grumble back.

"Oh, someone's in a bad mood," says Maddie with a smile, and Cassy laughs heartily too.

Without a word, I drag myself to the kitchenette and make myself a coffee.

"Is it your period that's making you suffer?" asks Cassy sympathetically.

I feel guilty about my lie and sigh.

"I lied to you yesterday. I'm fine. No cycle on the horizon!"

Maddie and Cassy look at me quizzically, their faces both curious and worried.

"During our dance, Lucas became intrusive. He followed me when I went to sit down, even though I wanted to put some distance between us. It was really scary... Then Liam saw fit to step in and make a scene," I continue.

"Wait... Liam? Like Liam Scott, the super-sexy captain of the hockey team?" asks Cassy, raising her eyebrows.

I nod.

Icebound Attraction

"He didn't just intervene, in fact... He hit Lucas..." Maddie exclaims, wide-eyed.

"They were both separated by security guards. It was too much for me, so I decided to go home," I finish, hoping they won't ask me any more questions.

"Two sexy men fought over you, and you're only telling us now, like you're telling us about your trip to the library! Well, it's not as exciting to know that Lucas is a pervert and an asshole, though..." advances Cassy.

"You were having a good time and I didn't want to spoil your evening," I say, sipping my coffee.

Maddie looks at me skeptically.

"Why was it so important for Liam to protect you?" she asks, frowning.

"We've been seeing a lot of each other lately because of the articles I write, and we get on well. I guess he felt obliged to do it. And Lucas is the captain of the opposing team they beat in the last game. That must explain it..." I say, half-laughing.

No, I'm not lying, I'm just not telling the whole truth!

Maddie and Cassy exchange a glance and I shrug.

To change the subject, I ask how the evening went. Cassy launches into a long stream of words, but when she mentions Chase, I perk up. She'd already flirted with him at the café. But unlike her usual self, she doesn't dwell on the subject and continues her monologue.

At least they had a good time!

Another message from Liam makes my phone vibrate.

* *Em, we can talk, please?*

I raise my eyes to the sky. I'd almost forgotten about him! I type a reply before he continues to pester me.

You hit Lucas and you meddled in a matter that didn't concern you. I've got nothing to say to you.

I feel bad, because I don't know how my conversation with the other asshole would have ended if he hadn't intervened. But I don't want to give him the satisfaction of thinking he's the hero of the story.
His response follows within seconds.

* *I know... I'm sorry. I shouldn't have done that. Can we meet, please?*

I close my eyes and take a deep breath. Right now, I really don't want to.

* *Maybe tomorrow, I'll be in touch.*

After sending the message, I switch off my phone.
He apologized, of course, but I'm still angry.

★★★

The next evening, I decide to give in. I've been thinking about it all day and it's seriously starting to pollute my brain.
The best thing is for us to talk like responsible adults.
After texting Liam, I drive to his house and, a little nervously, knock on his door.
Memories of our evening in his dorm room flood my thoughts and my heart beats noticeably faster.
I shake my head. I really don't need this right now!
The door half-opens and Liam lets me in after we've soberly greeted each other. When I see the couch, images appear in my mind again.

Pull yourself together, Emily.

Liam sits down next to me and hands me a glass of water.

"Why did you have to get involved? Lucas was a bit insistent, yes, but that's no reason to break his nose. Not to mention that I had the situation under control," I begin.

Liam sighs. I don't know if he has a guilty conscience, but he seems to.

"I couldn't help myself. When I saw you with him, I thought you were doing what you wanted, after all, we were clear about our relationship. But then I noticed that he was insistent and that you were trying to distance yourself. Despite that, he touched you, and that's when I went off the deep end..." he explains.

I breathe deeply, my feelings still in turmoil.

"But you could have left it at that. That didn't give you the right to behave like a madman and take advantage of it to settle your ego issues with him."

He frowns.

"What do you mean my ego problems? Do you really think that all that mattered at that moment was getting him to shut up because we'd clashed before on the ice? You've got it all wrong, Emily."

Now it's my turn to frown.

"The guy's an asshole, period. Yeah, I handled it wrong, and violence is a long way from solving everything. But his behavior crosses too many lines. Fuck, you said no! And it's always the same with him... He needed a beating," he continues.

There's a moment of silence between us, and I can feel my anger slowly fading.

"I understand, yes..."

I look up and meet his eyes. He seems to be seething inside.

"Honestly, what kind of guy would I have been if I hadn't intervened? Yes, I know you could have taken care of yourself that you're independent in that way. But who the hell would I have been if he'd dragged you into a corner to hurt you, huh?"

He seems genuinely upset and I'm touched by what I read in him.

"I..." I stammer.

He cuts me off.

"I care about you, Em. I really do. I'd do it all over again. Well, maybe this time I wouldn't break his nose..."

"Are you going to get into trouble because of this?" I ask, suddenly worried.

He shrugs.

For a moment, we say nothing.

I'm beginning to realize that our relationship is far more complicated than a normal friendship.

I nod and a feeling of reconciliation spreads between us.

★★★

The smell of freshly brewed coffee wafts through the air as Cassy and I enter the campus coffee shop.

Liam is seated at a table in a corner, with a blonde next to him. They're obviously having fun together and chatting animatedly.

My mood darkens instantly, and I hate having so little control over myself. Cassy notices my distraction and follows my gaze curiously.

"Checking out your knight in shining armor?"

I force myself to smile.

"No, don't be silly!" I evade. "I was just thinking."

In fact, I'm overcome by a feeling I don't know, like some kind of anxiety.

Could it be jealousy?

The way Liam laughs and talks to her tightens my stomach

and turns my heart inside out. Shit... I've never been jealous. I find it a terribly unnecessary feeling.

Cassy leans toward me.

"Would you like a cup of coffee?"

I jump.

"Yes, perfect! Thank you so much!"

Our conversation distracts me from Liam and his companion.

I keep glancing briefly over my shoulder, however, and see Liam embracing the beautiful blonde.

A new wave of jealousy washes over me.

Rha! Go away, you horrible feeling!

After our coffees, pastries and quick chats, Cassy bids me farewell and heads off to her class. As for me, I head for the library. I've got to write the article on the last game and I can't waste any more time.

Today, it's relatively empty. That's a pity. The soft murmur of people around me always helps me to concentrate on my work. I sit down at a table with my documents and laptop in front of me, ready to launch into my work.

But even with the best will in the world, I can't concentrate. The image of Liam and the blonde keeps looping in my head. They seemed so intimate with each other, as if there was something between them...

Silly girl! There must have been something between them! Liam has a reputation and you're just another number on his list.

I sigh in frustration, lean back and close my eyes for a moment.

After all, I'm the one who put distance between us. And obviously, he doesn't want a relationship right now either, or at least he can't afford one. But at the same time, he defended me and said he cared about me, right?

Damn it...

I had hoped that working at the library would help me get my head in order and distract me from my feelings, but the opposite seems to be happening. Every time I try to start a sentence of my article, I stall. I can literally feel the sting of jealousy attacking my heart, the questions looping around me, and I hate how much it affects me.

Suddenly, a hand rests on my shoulder, startling me, and when I look up, Maddie is next to me.

"Hey, what's up, sweetie?" she asks me softly.

I sigh again and shake my head.

"I can't concentrate on my article at all."

Maddie sits down next to me and smiles encouragingly.

"Sometimes it's hard to clear your head, especially when you're battling thoughts of all kinds."

I nod in agreement.

"Yes... I thought the library would help me."

But it reminds me even more of Liam...

She places a comforting hand on my arm.

"What's on your mind?"

I hesitate for a moment before telling her everything.

My conversations with Liam, our study sessions, our night, then our agreement, my feelings getting tangled, my jealousy...

Maddie opens her eyes wide and hiccups in surprise at times, but she lets me empty my bag. Once I've finished, I look up at her in shame. She's my best friend, and yet I've kept all this from her.

"Wow... Emily... Wow!" she exclaims, as if shocked.

"I'm sorry, I should have told you."

"Don't apologize! You're entitled to a secret garden too! You agreed not to tell anyone about your study sessions. Well, I didn't expect you to tell me you'd slept with Liam Scott. And it sounded really hot!"

I blush in spite of myself.

"But you don't owe me anything, and I'm glad you decided to talk to me about it. I get the impression that it's weighing on you a lot..." she finishes.

She pats my arm, sympathetic, and I sigh.

"I hate feeling this way..."

"Jealousy is a natural emotion. It's important to recognize it and understand where it comes from. And above all, why it occurs."

I massage my forehead.

"But I don't want jealousy to rule my thoughts and actions," I declare.

She smiles softly.

"Instead of repressing it, try to understand it. Why are you jealous?"

I think about it for a moment.

"I wonder if that evening with me meant anything to him."

Maddie takes my hand in hers.

"These thoughts are normal, but you should also realize that you are precious and unique. And you're the one who suggested the two of you should be friends. If that's not what you want, you have to tell him. But if you think it's the best thing for both of you, then *really* become friends."

I didn't tell Maddie about the conversation I overheard between Liam and Coach Franklyn. And more importantly, why I went to talk to him in the first place. One thing at a time, and I've already made some big revelations.

"Thank you, Maddie. You're right, I shouldn't let someone psych me out like that."

"You're a strong, independent woman!" she says, encouraging me. "And I'm here for you if you ever need to talk."

I hug Maddie and feel my determination grow.

It's time for me to pull myself together and stop letting my emotions rule me. I'll never get far in life if I have an emotional crisis after every one-night stand.

Maddie is simply incredible. She always knows what to say. Sometimes I feel like she knows me better than I know myself.

After she leaves, I'm off for a walk around campus. A little distraction will do me good, and maybe I'll find the words to write my column.

With my camera in hand, I wander around campus, taking photos of anything that catches my eye. I like to immortalize the everyday and the little details of life. It helps me shift focus when I feel like I'm trapped in my own head.

As I squat in front of a tree and adjust my aim, I notice Chase doing some stretching exercises on a bench.

He smiles at me, and I smile back. I approach him and we chat a little. What a nice guy! Cassy is right to fall for him: he's open, kind and, let's face it, really hot!

Suddenly, I feel a shadow looming over me and, looking up, I see Liam standing beside us. The expression on his face is hard to interpret.

"Hey! Emily, can I talk to you for a minute?" he asks, his voice serious.

I bite my lip and suddenly feel uncomfortable.

"Of course!" I reply, feigning detachment.

Without a word, I walk away to a quieter spot. When we stop, I can feel the tension in the air between us.

"What is it?" I finally ask, my voice trying to relax.

We observe each other for a moment. Liam seems to be deep in thought. I see his gaze drift from my eyes to my mouth, and suddenly he closes the distance between us to place his lips on mine.

Caught off guard, I can't push him away and feel myself engulfed by the kiss I've been hoping for with all my heart.

Red alert! Red alert!

10

Liam

I know Chase would never hit on Emily because he suspects there's something between us. He keeps trying to get it out of me. I stand my ground! This guy is good with his questions and his innocent air. But still, when I see the two of them laughing, having a good time, and above all looking like they're confiding in each other, my blood runs cold. I feel like Emily is slipping away from me, and I want to be the one she can do all that with.

So, when we're alone, I can't contain myself, and when I kiss her, everything makes sense.

Her lips are incredibly soft and warm. It's as if the world around us stops. It's not just desire, passion, ardor, it's deeper, more meaningful.

I take her face in my hands and slowly withdraw. She looks up at me with her big blue eyes, filled with surprise and other emotions I can't quite put my finger on.

"Liam..." she whispers. "You... We can't..."

I swallow my own confusion.

"I'm sorry," I mumble, and without asking for more, I take off.

Suddenly, I feel vulnerable, and all I want to do is go home.

The darkness of my room envelops me as I lie on my bed, my thoughts swirling like a storm. The events of the last few days have swept me up in a tsunami of emotions, and I can't find peace in my own head.

Emily...

Her name echoes in me. I remember her eyes, her lips, the way she laughs. But in the midst of these memories, there's also a truth I can no longer ignore. I'm fighting against myself, caught between my desire to be with her and the ambitions I have for my career.

That kiss turned my emotions upside down. Emily touches me in a way I never expected. What the hell? We both decided we'd better be friends. Well... Her, more than me... But she was right! And yet, here I am - confused, upset and distracted.

I sigh, staring at the ceiling.

Emily or my career?

I feel like I have to choose between an arm and a leg. And whichever way I choose, there will be consequences.

I try to imagine what it would be like not to see Emily at all, to avoid her, to ignore her, to cut her out of my life. Just thinking about it terrifies me - as if I had to give up an important part of my life.

Can I afford to have a relationship while advancing my career? Can I reconcile the two without conflict? Is love really an obstacle to becoming a professional? Some people have done it, haven't they?

I'm trying to think of all the professional players I know who are happily married.

Dude, do you think you're looking at a celebrity magazine? And we're talking about a relationship, not marriage, get off!

And yet, she encourages me firm in my studies, anchors me in my daily life, pushes me and always sees the best in me. She knows a thing or two about hockey now! What more could you ask for? Should I open up to her about all this?

I rub my forehead.

But Emily has her own dreams and goals, she's made that clear, and I don't want to hold her back in any way.

Damn.

My reflections are meaningless, since she did set limits.

I close my eyes and try to calm down a little.

Maybe I just need a little time to figure out exactly what I want... There's no point in boning her and then running away. What a jerk...

★★★

The next day, I'm supposed to meet her for our study session, but the mood is overshadowed by our kiss and, above all, my hasty escape. I can't even look Emily in the eye. However, I notice that, against all odds, she has come.

The feeling that she, too, would like more than friendship keeps creeping into my head. Am I kidding myself that we have a chance?

Meanwhile, Emily tries to explain a class note to me, but I just don't get it.

After about half an hour, as she patiently repeats herself, I interrupt her:

"Sorry, I can't concentrate. It doesn't make sense. Can we stop for today?"

Her blue eyes look up at me.

"If you prefer, yes. It's fine with me actually, I've got stuff to do..."

Already, she's gathering her things as if it's too good an opportunity to get the hell out of here and, in turn, away from me. That's all I deserve, after all.

"See you tomorrow, Liam."

I watch her leave the library and rest my head on the table in front of me.

It really can't go on like this. Maybe I could talk to Chase after practice... After all, he knows me best and might be able to advise me.

The feel of the ice under my skates is pleasant, and the sound of my glides echoes softly in my ears. However, I'm not at my best and I can feel my teammates tightening around me.

My shots are weak, my passes uncertain, and I'm making mistakes I didn't even make when I was starting out.

"Focus, Liam!" shouts Coach Franklyn, his voice urgent, but barely seeming to pierce the fog in my head.

I can feel the pressure on me - as a captain, as a player who's normally reliable. But today, I'm not.

Brad, a defender, approaches me, a snide expression on his face.

"Is it Lucas Stern's blood-pissing nose that's still got you going?"

My cheeks heat up and I feel anger rising inside me.

"Shut up, Brad."

"Or else what? The captain will jump down my throat?"

He laughs, pleased with his joke, and I feel piqued. Chase intervenes just in time, nudging me back to the side of the rink with the flat of his hand.

"Easy, Liam. He's just looking for you..."

Coach Franklyn is watching us, and I'd rather take off my skates than continue training, at the risk of hitting someone.

"For God's sake, Liam, what's happened to you? Your altercation with Stern, and now this?"

He scratches the back of his neck, annoyed.

"Sorry, coach. I'm going to get some fresh air, and tomorrow I'll be fine."

"You know I went to a lot of trouble to make sure you didn't get called into the administration office. Stern deserved it, right, I have no doubt about that, the guy's a jerk. But still... think about your file."

Yes, I know, and my future.

"Duly noted, coach."

I can't say anything else, and I'd rather withdraw.

★★★

The air in the park has cooled and the street lights have already been on for a while, when Chase approaches me with a smile.

I hope he can give me some advice. He's someone who knows a lot about women's issues, as well as men's, and may have another perspective on my situation.

He smiles encouragingly as he sits down next to me.

"Feeling better?"

Lying on the lawn, I sit up on my elbows and grimace.

"Thanks for earlier. Brad got on my nerves..."

"I get the impression that right now, you're pretty much on edge," he says.

"I can't stop thinking about a lot of stuff, yeah, and it's starting to show."

Chase frowns.

"Does it have anything to do with Emily?"

I nod.

"It's really complicated. I think that..."

I hesitate for a moment, struggling to put it into words. Especially out loud.

"I think I really like her," I finally say.

"No kidding!"

Chase bursts out laughing, and I look at him surprised.

"Fuck, is it that obvious?" I exclaim, a little offended.

"Because I know you. Don't worry, the others just think you're grumpy at the moment, that's all."

I sigh.

"I just don't know how to deal with it. On the one hand, I want to get closer to Emily, but on the other, I'm afraid that a relationship would damage my career. The coach has talked my ear off about this so much!"

Chase nods slowly.

"It's not an easy decision. But I think it's important to be honest with yourself and find out what you really want. Franklyn or not."

I stare up at the dark sky, thoughts still swirling in my head.

"I feel like I'm between two worlds: Emily and ice hockey. To think that I used to try to reconcile studies and sport, and now feelings are getting in the way. Fucking temptations!" I exclaim.

Chase wraps his arms around his knees before speaking.

"And why shouldn't they be part of the same world? You think too much about the two things you like, seeing them as two different entities."

I think for a moment before answering.

"I want to be with Emily, while pursuing my goals."

Chase smiles gently.

"Well, you see, you're making progress! It might not be easy, but if you're prepared to invest time and effort in both areas, you might find a way to reconcile them. Emily's also helping you with your lessons, so she's not going to be the one to upset you in that respect - in fact, since you've been seeing her, you've improved a lot!"

"But how can I be sure that I won't regret my choices later?"

Chase raises an eyebrow and laughs.

"Dude, if you find the answer, tell me! That's what makes a choice difficult most of the time. But, sometimes, you have to take risks. Above all, you should talk to Emily about your feelings, your fears, your goals. Maybe together you can find a way that works for both of you."

"If she wants me! She keeps throwing the word 'friendship' in my face..."

"You're not helping her with your attitude."

"You're right..."

Chase smiles and punches me in the shoulder.

"It's going to be great!"

As we continue chatting, my thoughts gradually clear up. I still don't know exactly what I should do, but at least I feel better equipped to face the challenges ahead.

One thing's for sure: I have to talk to Emily.

★★★

I bite my lower lip nervously. In a few minutes, Emily will be at my door.

The sun is already approaching the horizon and I'm desperately trying to stay calm. When she knocks, my heart almost leaps out of my chest - she's here.

We say hello, and she passes me by, leaving in her wake the perfume I love so much. Fruit, spring, sunshine. I invite her to sit down, and it feels like a repeat of last time.

Tension immediately builds between us. I look at her briefly before sitting down next to her. Taking a deep breath, I gather all my strength and begin to speak.

"I've been doing a lot of thinking lately. I've had a few bad days at training and I've been feeling a bit under the weather. I realized I had to make a decision."

Emily watches me with curiosity and apprehension. She lets me continue.

"Emily, you really mean a lot to me. The time we spend together, our studying, our exchanges, our..."

I refrain from saying 'kisses'.

"I realize that you're taking up more and more space in my mind," I continue, my voice hoarser than I'd like it to be. "I know we said we'd be 'friends', but I just can't do it. You're... You're always in the back of my mind."

I drop it like a bomb. I don't think I really put it into words, but it had to come out.

Her eyes open in surprise and her mouth rounds.

"I wanted to tell you, because I had to be honest and let you know why I run away most of the time. Not because I'm making fun of you, no. It's the opposite actually. Because you mean so much to me, despite the limits you've set."

A moment's silence follows my words, and I see her eyes light up. I'm suddenly filled with hope. That everything I'm feeling is mutual.

Am I to deduce that her famous limits were a bluff?

She swallows before answering.

"That's... quite a statement!"

I lower my eyes and my heart tightens, waiting for what comes next. Maybe... maybe I really am just a friend? That would be hard to hear, but at least I'll be able to move on.

Unexpectedly, her hand rests gently on mine, and I raise my eyes to look into hers.

"Liam, I can't get used to the idea that we're just friends either. I just can't..."

"Do you want us to stop seeing each other, then?" I formulate slowly.

"No! Idiot! I... I want more!"

She blushes. A blush I love more than anything. I grab her

hand and a warm shiver runs down my back.

"Emily, I do believe I'm falling for you. Me, who's never had a stable relationship. Me, who always dismissed it with a wave of my hand."

A ball of emotion forms in my throat.

Crap. Is this what love is?

"And I think I'm falling for you too. Dealing with my feelings was too difficult, which is why I suggested we be friends, but even that... I couldn't do it. I wanted to come and tell you one night after your training session, but I overheard you and the coach. He was telling you that nothing should interfere with your goals."

"But you won't get in my way; on the contrary, without you, I can't concentrate."

She smiles and places her lips on mine. We kiss softly, slowly, sweetly, like a first real kiss. There's this connection that ignites between us, and our bodies instinctively move closer together. It's as if we can finally let go of something real and strong.

Her hands slide over me, down my shirt, greedy, curious, and I do the same, eventually throwing her top across the room. She reaches into my little condom basket herself to grab one, which makes me smile. She's remembered my hiding place! This time, we get up together and move to my bed, to a cozier nest to share another moment of ecstasy together.

With our clothes off, I gaze at her, my dick stiff with excitement. Her thighs are offered, her breasts, her graceful body, and her intimacy just waiting for me. Once the condom is on, I slide into her with ease, hearing her moan in my ear.

These little cries are enough to make me lose my mind and I start to thrust into her faster and harder. Her legs wrap around my hips and she pushes her pelvis towards me. Our rhythm matches, intense, and our skins start to glisten with sweat.

It's fucking good. This is really good.

I come and go, giving her no respite, and she ends up biting a cushion so as not to panic my neighbors with her screams. I pound into her with force, feeling the walls of her sex absorb me. It's as if we were made for each other.

Suddenly, I feel her tipping over, she gasps harder, squeezes my shoulders, and it turns me on even more. My pleasure increases and we cum in unison, letting ourselves fall back against each other.

I want this every day…

11

Emily

When my lips meet Liam's, it's as if the earth moves beneath my feet. His kiss stirs my soul.

After our torrid embrace, we slowly catch our breath and look at each other. A laugh escapes me. It's so good to be together again, to share this moment together! The pressure off, the fears gone, the doubts erased, I sleep like never before in the arms of the man I'm in love with.

The next morning, I emerge slowly, stretching out before I remember where I am. For a moment, I watch him sleep, observing his chest as it rises and falls to the rhythm of his peaceful breathing.

"Emily, I can feel you looking at me..." he mumbles.

He smiles, a dazzling smile that transports me.

Then suddenly, he grabs me and pulls me against him. I feel his erection against the sheet that separates us. My heart misses a beat and, immediately, shivers run through my body again. With a mischievous grin, I slide astride him, pulling back the covers that separates us.

"Hello there," he murmurs as he takes me against him.

I look around, searching for protection. This guy is very organized when it comes to sex, I'm sure he has condoms by his bed.

"Bedside table," he laughs, as if reading my mind.

I open the drawer and unroll a string of condoms, trying not to dwell on the fact that this equipment means he is very sexually active, and take one.

Meticulously, I set about slipping it onto his stiffened dick, and he lets me, watching me with a particularly sexy air. No sooner have I finished than he grabs me by the hips and penetrates me. A feeling of passion fills me. I bite him on the shoulder to keep from moaning too loudly. It's just too good. I grab his mid-length hair and free his neck so I can plunge my mouth in to bite him gently.

"You're incredibly sexy in the morning," he whispers in my ear, making me shiver.

"And you're incredibly handsome."

He laughs, and I start to move my hips at a slow pace. This time, I'm in no hurry; I want to enjoy the feel of him inside me and explore his body. My hands roam over his muscular arms and well-developed torso. And I lean in to kiss him passionately.

Just as another orgasm is about to begin, he lifts me off him and flips me flat on my back on the mattress. There, on my back, I feel the warmth of his body, and he takes me from behind before I've even had a chance to exhale.

This angle allows him to hit a crucial point deep inside me, which almost makes me explode. I grab hold of the sheets and push my butt towards him to keep going. It's as if he knows exactly what I need and what I like. After several incandescent minutes, we rush over the cliff together and free ourselves.

The intensity of our feelings and the wild passion have exhausted us both. We lie side by side on the bed, our breathing only slowly normalizing as we feel the after-effects of this intense moment.

Liam's gaze is fixed on me and intense emotions flutter in his eyes - love, desire and deep complicity. His hand gently caresses my skin, and a smile stretches his lips.

"Emily," he murmurs, his voice even huskier than before.

I turn my head towards him and smile back.

"Yes?"

He hesitates a moment before speaking.

"I'm as hungry as a wolf. Shall we order something to eat?"

I burst out laughing and nod. Liam grabs his cell phone with a smile and orders Chinese food for us.

While waiting for the delivery, we chat about everything and anything. The conversation flows effortlessly, as if we'd never parted. We talk about our dreams, but also about little anecdotes from our lives.

The hours tick by like seconds and it's suddenly late at night.

I think I just spent a day naked making love to Liam Scott.

"I can't believe what time it is," I finally say, yawning.

Liam laughs softly.

"Time flies when you're in good company."

I smile and snuggle up to him.

The darkness that surrounds us creates a kind of cocoon of intimacy that protects our closeness like a special treasure. His smile is gentle and affectionate as he gently squeezes my hand.

"I want you to stay with me tonight, Emily."

My heart leaps with happiness and a warm feeling comes over me.

"I'd love to stay with you, but if I spend one more night here, Maddie and Cassy will call the FBI and put out an APB."

We both laugh and he pulls me closer to kiss me on the forehead. The warmth of our bodies mingles and I sigh with satisfaction.

"All right," he finally says, pouting slightly.

As much as I'd love to stay, I really need to get home. It's not a bad idea to let it all settle down, take a shower too, put on some clothes, and see how we can reconcile our new relationship with our obligations and passions.

A vast program...

Liam looks at me and gently strokes my cheek.

"What's on your mind?"

I hesitate for a moment before answering.

"Us. I think it's best if we don't announce our relationship just yet. I don't want to be known as the girlfriend of the most attractive ice hockey captain on campus before I've made a name for myself as a sportswriter. And I don't want anyone to think I gave you an advantage in my articles because I'm with you. My integrity is important. Besides, I think it would be better for you too... Don't you?"

Memories of Liam's conversation with Coach Franklyn appear in my mind.

I bite my lip; afraid I've gone too far with my suggestion. But it's important to be honest if we want this to work.

Liam's gaze turns serious and he takes my hand in his.

"I agree. Rumors could have a negative effect on both of us. And right now, I want us to enjoy what we have without having to worry about other people's opinions. I don't want to hide you, don't get me wrong!"

I nod.

"I don't want to hide you either, but it would be wiser. And I really should be getting home now!" I say with determination after a few seconds.

Liam grabs my face and forces me to look at him, trapping my eyes in his.

"Whatever happens, remember that I want to be with you."

My heart beats faster with joy and I kiss him. The kiss is intense and quickly becomes passionate. But before we can undress each other again, I push Liam away, laughing.

I'm very bad at hiding things, but I have to go through this. I hope I can keep my distance to protect us both.

★★★

A familiar scent greets me as I push open my bedroom door. It smells of cinnamon and spices. I breathe it in, happy.

I really feel safe here.

Cassy is once again sliding vases, floral arrangements and candlesticks onto a piece of furniture. She examines her decoration, her head cocked to one side.

"Hi, desert girl! Were you at Maddie's last night? How did it go?" she asks almost casually.

I feel my heartbeat quicken.

Under normal circumstances, I could answer that question without a problem. But today, I have a secret to keep - something I can't share with Cassy yet. She could never keep it to herself and I don't want to take any chances.

"Uh... I..."

Don't stammer, Emily!

Cassy turns to me and frowns, waiting for the next part.

"I fell asleep at the newspaper office!" I finally exclaim, trying not to put Maddie on the spot.

"That's why you look so tired!" she says with her usual tact.

I breathe a sigh of relief.

"Yes, I had a backlog of articles and research to do. The day flew by at breakneck speed and I'm only going home now."

She continues to stare at me, and I can literally see her mind at work. I hate lying to her, but I have to go through this.

"You're working too hard!" she finally replies, even though her face looks as skeptical as ever.

"Yeah, I know," I nod. "But don't worry about me!"

She nods slowly and seems to believe me. Relieved that she doesn't insist, I breathe. But at the same time, I feel bad that I can't tell her the truth.

As I shower and get ready for bed, a lump forms in my stomach. I've always had trouble lying and I wonder how long Liam and I will have to keep our happiness to ourselves.

★★★

The atmosphere in the campus newspaper office is always lively - the clatter of keyboards, the murmur of conversations and the rustle of papers form a background noise that takes some getting used to.

Sitting at my desk, I'm lost in thought.

My budding relationship with Liam is really perfect. We still meet at lunchtime to study together, and often escape between two shelves of books for more 'in-depth studying'.

Just goes to show, I'll end up getting laid in that library too!

In the evenings, after his training, we continue our studies together. It's either the books that absorb us, or the other's body. But we still manage to balance our busy lives. Our feelings don't erase our responsibilities and goals, and that's what I love about us. We're aware of each other's expectations of our careers, and so far, so good. Liam's grades are even excellent!

Maddie and Cassy did notice that I haven't been very available lately, but they put that down to my tendency to study a lot.

If they only knew...

And it's true that I feel guilty letting them think that when I'm having the time of my life.

Suddenly, the landline next to me rings and I touch my heart, startled. Nobody ever calls me here. I look at the display and recognize a New York number.

Icebound Attraction

Curious, I pick up the phone.

"Hello?"

"Hello, am I speaking to... Emily Hansen?" The female voice on the other end of the line sounds professional.

"Yes, that's me," I reply.

"Perfect! My name is Laura Johnson from the *New York Post*. We've been reading about your university's ice hockey team and are very impressed with your work. We'd like to offer you the opportunity to intern with us."

I can hardly believe my ears. The *New York Post* - one of the city's most prestigious newspapers - wants to offer me an internship? What an incredible opportunity!

"Oh, thank you so much! I'm honored!" I exclaim, unable to contain my enthusiasm. "Thank you for this opportunity," I continue, trying to sound a little more professional.

"We're convinced you can be an asset to our team," replies Ms. Johnson. "Can you drop by our office this lunchtime for an interview? I'm sorry to spring this on you, but we'd like to confirm this with you as soon as possible."

I swallow hard, my heart rate quickens and my hands become clammy.

I'm meeting Liam for lunch.

I bite my lip, my thoughts swirling. The opportunity to intern at the *New York Post* is too tempting to pass up. I'm sure he'll understand!

"Yes, no problem," I finally say.

"Perfect! Then we'll see you at noon in our offices."

The call ends and I sit in silence for a moment.

It's absolutely crazy!

I grab my phone and type a quick message to Liam to let him know.

* Hi there! I'm so sorry, but we'll have to postpone our lunch date. I'll explain!

I'm deliberately not giving him any more details so as not to jinx myself if I don't get in. I hope he won't be offended that I canceled in the morning, and that he'll be happy for me when I tell him everything.

I have just enough time to go back to my room, change and get out of here. My thoughts turn to this professional opportunity and, at the same time, I worry about the impact it could have on my life.

Will I have enough time for my private life?

My excitement is barely bearable when I slip on matching pants and blazer.

Cassy came over to help me when I texted the girls to let them know. She hands me a coffee and smiles encouragingly.

"You're worrying for nothing, Emily. It's going to be fine!"

I sigh.

"It's a huge opportunity and I want to make a good impression!"

She nods and looks at me.

"What you've chosen is perfect!"

For once, she validates my outfit, and that's something to set in stone!

I smile gratefully.

"And you're going to rock this interview," she says with a wink.

The journey to the *New York Post* office seems interminable, and my nervousness grows with every step. Thousands of people are milling about in the streets, and the city's hustle and bustle reverberates inside me. When I finally reach the front of the building, I take a deep breath.

I sign in at reception and take the opportunity to look around. The atmosphere is electric, smelling of paper all the way down the hall.

When I'm asked to climb the stairs, I feel like I'm going to faint.

Yet the interview goes surprisingly well. The people present are professional and friendly, and my nervousness diminishes as I talk about my experience and passion for journalism.

"We were impressed by your articles, Emily," says one of the journalists opposite me. "We read student newspapers with great interest to find rare gems like you. We're used to meeting our trainees, which is why we contacted you directly. And we think you'd be an excellent addition to our team."

The words ring in my ears and my heart beats with excitement. This is more than I expected.

"I... thank you very much," I reply, my voice trembling slightly.

Once the formalities have been completed, I leave the office with a smile on my face. I take a deep breath and observe the bustle of the city for a moment. The streets of New York suddenly seem brighter, full of possibilities and opportunities. And I'm ready to seize them all.

Once back on campus, I immediately grab my cell phone and text Maddie to let her know I've got the job. Then I also text Liam to explain in more detail what it's all about. His reply warms my heart and I'm relieved he's taking it this way.

* *Em! It's fantastic! I'm really happy for you!* <3

But at the same time, a thought pops into my head: accepting the internship means that I'll have to devote even more time to my professional career. I made this decision without thinking too much about it - the opportunity was too good to turn down. But now I'm wondering what impact this new step will have on my relationship with Liam.

I hope I'll be able to reconcile everything.

★★★

The next day, I join the rink, excited. An article about the team is being written for the university newspaper, and I want to gather enough information to write a great article.

But as I watch the training, I can't turn my thoughts away from Liam.

How attractive he is when he is sweating and working out... Immediately, confusing images take hold of me, and I tighten my grip on my notebook.

The way Liam glides across the ice, with the passion and energy he puts into every movement, is incredibly sexy. It's hard not to run to him and hug him. But our relationship is still a secret we want to keep, and I pull myself together.

Time flies and when the players leave the ice, I'm sure I'll have enough material to complete my article.

Liam takes advantage of the fact that his teammates are in the changing rooms to glide over to me, the sweat on his forehead glistening in the sunlight streaming through a window.

"Hey," he says, smiling.

"Hey," I reply with the same smile.

My heart races as he approaches.

"Did you like what you saw?" he asks with a mischievous grin.

My cheeks are getting hot.

"As always... But they were professional observations, you know."

I shake my notebook, laughing, and his smile widens.

"Well... I can't wait to read your new article."

The butterflies in my stomach take flight and swirl in all directions. It's so hard not to jump on him right away!

I wait for him to finish showering, and together we leave the rink for a bite to eat.

As we sit in a café close to campus and chat, I think to myself that time spent with Liam feels familiar and natural. I'm really enjoying it. My decision to accept the internship at the *New York Post* weighs all the more heavily.

Suddenly, a lump forms in my throat.

Liam notices my silence.

"Are you okay, Em?"

I force a smile to my lips.

"Yes, everything's fine!"

But his eyes pierce me. I sigh and finally let go.

"I'm afraid we won't find the time to see each other anymore and we'll drift apart when I start my internship."

Liam puts his hand on mine and forces me to look at him.

"Hey, it's gonna be okay, all right? Don't you worry about a thing. We'll find a way to make it work. We're stronger than this. Besides, our dreams are important, too."

His words calm me down a little, allowing me to look up and appreciate his beautiful smile. So much sex appeal in one person shouldn't be allowed. My knees soften as his hand caresses mine and my whole body begins to tingle.

His eyes. His lips...

My throat suddenly becomes dry and I feel as if I'm about to burst into a thousand pieces. When I can't stand the tension any longer, I pretend I need to go to the toilet for a change of air.

"Get a grip, Emily! Puberty's long over," I say to myself, looking at myself in the mirror.

Suddenly the door opens behind me, and Liam enters.

"What are you..."

I don't have time to finish my sentence before he locks the main door behind him. His eyes are dark with desire, his lips slightly parted, and to see him like this takes my excitement up a notch. He turns me against the wall and starts kissing my neck.

Little electric shocks tickle my skin and my body bursts into flames.

With an air of determination, Liam pushes us into one of the cubicles. Without wasting any time, he puts his hand under my short dress, finds my panties and pulls them down. It's a good thing I'm not wearing tights on this hot day, and once his condom is on, he can penetrate me straight away.

"Huuuum..." I groan.

It's as if something explodes inside me.

He takes me hard and fast, with an urgency that catches me completely off guard.

In a very short time, we reach a climax together and when Liam pulls away, I feel empty. I want more, more of this, more of him.

Without saying a word, he winks at me and leaves, taking my underwear with him. At the door, he removes the bolt and turns around one last time.

"As a souvenir," he says mischievously, shaking my panties.

What the...

I'm standing in front of the toilet, legs shaking and breathless, still wondering what just happened.

It was so hot!

When I finally come out, Liam is sitting at our table sipping his beer as if he hasn't just fucked me in a public toilet.

I try to calm down and sit down opposite him. The sensation of not wearing underwear turns me on more than I care to admit, but I pull myself together.

The rest of our meal together is spent in pleasant conversation, and I try to put aside my thoughts about the future. The love I feel for Liam is very special, and I'm sure we'll find ways to preserve our relationship.

As we leave the café and head towards Liam's university building, I can't help but grab his hand repeatedly, only to let go as soon as we see someone. I want to devour him right here on campus... I push him back and exchange an intense kiss with him.

Our bond is strong, full of passion and understanding - it's something I won't give up, no matter how complicated the future may be.

We're on our way again when we spot Coach Franklyn. Instinctively, we take a step away from each other.

"Liam! And Emily..."

He looks at us skeptically but adds nothing.

My gaze shifts from Liam to the coach before I hastily take my leave.

I hope he didn't see anything...

12

Liam

The quickie in the bathroom stall was truly amazing. I can't wait to seduce Emily back into my bed! There are so many things I want to try with her.

But when we get close to my place, after exchanging the promise of a torrid night, her greedy mouth against mine, we cross paths with the coach.

Shit...

Emily quickly runs off, clearly uncomfortable, and the coach gives me a piercing look.

My naughty evening just fell through.

"Coach, have you lost your way?"

His attention then turns to Emily, who is striding away, before returning to me. A small flush of anxiety passes through me and, suddenly, I'm nervous.

"I hope I haven't upset your plans for the evening," he says.

"No, of course not!" I reply quickly. "We've just finished studying together, and I was taking her home."

"Ha? I thought we were near your university building here..."

He makes a little pout that doesn't bode well.

"I was coming to see you to talk about the next game," he

explains. "I tried to call you, but you didn't answer, and the situation is urgent."

That's right, I remember putting my phone on silent and completely forgetting about it for the duration of my tête-à-tête.

I nod, waiting for the next part.

"Logan is injured. After training, he had pain in his right leg, and it turns out that his knee was badly bruised. He won't be on skates for the next game."

I whistle through my teeth.

Logan is a striker, and he does a great job. I often rely on him to score.

"It sucks..." I whisper.

"And an important scout will be present at the game the day after tomorrow. I think it's a great opportunity to show you off. However, it's going to be a bit difficult without Logan. As captain, who would you trust most to replace him?"

My heart leaps and relief spreads.

A scout. This means that my performance in this game will be of particular importance. A feeling of excitement mingles with the pressure suddenly weighing on my shoulders.

"The best would be Mark. I can communicate well with him. He's quick and attentive. And... Coach, I'll do my best."

Coach Franklyn nods with satisfaction.

"That's exactly what I want from you, Liam. The match is in two days. Make sure you're well prepared. We may have to add an extra workout with Mark to get you coordinated," he ponders aloud.

"I'll make sure we're both in tip-top shape."

The coach nods with satisfaction.

"I like the sound of that. You have to work hard, Liam, you know that?"

"As hard as I can," I answer with determination.

"I hope you won't let yourself be distracted by some woman... This game could be decisive for your career," he says before strolling away, leaving me alone with my fears.

★★★

Time flies as I immerse myself in the exercises, my mind entirely focused on the game ahead. From fitness exercises to skating to shooting practice, every spare minute is devoted to an extra workout to keep Mark and me in top shape.

But this intensive preparation also means that I don't have much time for anything else.

I keep reaching for my cell phone to let Emily know I'm thinking of her. But every time I see the screen, I remind myself that I don't have time for distractions. I'm focused on the game, on my career - and I have to make sure I don't let anything slip through the cracks to achieve my goals. Emily will understand.

On the day of the game, the excitement is like a rollercoaster in my body. The locker room is filled with a mixture of tension and anticipation as we prepare for the battle ahead. Coach Franklyn says a few words of motivation and we take possession of the rink.

This is where it all counts.

With my heart pounding, I stand on the ice, surrounded by my teammates, and I can feel the energy around me. It's as if the air is charged with electrical tension. The stands are full, eyes riveted on us, and I breathe deeply to calm myself.

The scout will be watching our every move and I'm ready to show him what I can do. Emily's eyes are on me too, and she gives me an encouraging nod.

Knowing that she's there to support me makes me feel better.

The game is intense. The action on the ice is a wild mix of rapid movement and strategy. Every shot, every decision, every move counts.

My team and I fight side by side, and I put my passion for ice hockey into every movement.

Minutes fly by like seconds, and we soon find ourselves in the game's final moments.

My breathing becomes heavy as I line up for the final kick-off. Time is running out and the score is tied. My hands shake with tension. Somewhere, high up in the stands, the scout is watching our every move, no matter how small. Everything seems to pass before me in slow motion.

The linesman throws the puck. I pick it up in a flash and go for it. The defenders try to parry it, but I dodge around them and fake a pass. I use the last of my strength to throw the puck towards the opposing net and watch the scene before me, fascinated.

The puck slips past the keeper and is trapped. I raise my arms, euphoria coursing through my veins.

We've won! I scored the decisive goal!

Maybe my dream is within reach.

And then the final whistle sounds and the game is over.

My heart beats furiously in my chest as I take off my helmet and look at the stands where the crowd is going wild. Emily flashes a big smile and Coach Franklyn gives me a thumbs-up. I can only hope I've shown what I'm capable of, and that the scout liked what he saw.

We leave the ice and the locker room is filled with mixed emotions. The joy of victory, fatigue, excitement, hope - all reflected on the faces of my teammates.

I'm proud of what we've achieved together, but at the same time, uncertainty sets in. Have we done enough to impress the recruiter present?

"Great game, guys! I'm proud of you!" I declare loudly, tapping them on the shoulder.

As the commotion subsides and I leave to go home, I can't help thinking about Emily. We agreed to meet at my place tonight, and I had to make up an excuse for the guys who wanted me to go partying with them.

Liam Scott's refusal to attend a party makes a lasting impression!

But I've missed the presence of my lovely blonde these past few days, and I can't wait to see her.

I'm convinced that my decision to concentrate on training was the right one, yet I must admit that not seeing her for forty-eight hours was difficult. My thoughts turn to the time we spent together, the moments of complicity and happiness.

I feel pulled in two different directions - towards my passion for hockey and my love for Emily. It's a complex balancing act.

Suddenly, I see her. She's waiting for me at my front door, a six-pack of beer in hand.

This woman is truly incredible!

"My captain!" she exclaims loudly, bowing.

As I approach her, laughing out loud, she applauds. I just shake my head. It's a side of her I particularly like. So carefree and happy, funny and adorable.

Immediately, images of our embrace in the coffee shop's bathroom rush into my head. I embrace her violently, and she instinctively wraps her legs around me. I carry her up the stairs to my apartment. She laughs heartily and kisses my neck as I unlock my door.

My pants start to tighten around my crotch, and I drop her on the bed without warning before literally throwing myself on top of her. I kiss her passionately as I try to undress her. As much as I want to go slowly, my body has other plans. I want her right now.

I help her out of her tight jeans, pull off my own clothes and kiss her. She's so sexy, her skin so soft. Emily squirms beneath me and moans loudly as I stop between her thighs. I lick her, suck her, devour her.

It tastes delicious.

"Liam," she murmurs, and the sound of her slightly deep voice only excites me more.

Without wasting any more time, I grab a condom and rush to penetrate her. We both sigh loudly.

To be united with her in this way is a divine sensation. I hold her by the neck with my right hand and slip my thumb into her mouth. She sucks and nibbles on it while my left hand holds her by the hip. After a few violent strokes, I have to stop to avoid cumming right away. I kiss her hungrily before turning her onto her stomach and penetrating her from behind. Emily rotates her hips and bites my pillow. This woman really drives me crazy. My fingers dig deep into her skin as I hold her by the shoulders and penetrate her deeper. Sweat breaks out on my forehead and I can't hold back any longer. With a few quick, hard strokes, I make us both come.

Out of breath and with a smile of satisfaction, I roll over and lie down next to her. She turns to me.

Her tousled hair, her rosy cheeks, her post-orgasm glow and her incredible, loving eyes... For quite a while, we just stand there looking at each other. There's something intimate and familiar about the silence.

I'd never want to be without it again.

I rub my eyes and stretch gently. Emily is still lying beside me. Her peaceful sleep is like a precious moment of calm in the midst of all the exciting events of late.

Her breathing is steady and I can't help but stare at her for a moment, fascinated by the beauty she exudes. I detach myself from her embrace and stand up as discreetly as possible.

Last night's perfume still lingers in the air, proof of the passion and closeness we shared. When I look in the bathroom mirror, I can't suppress a smile. My hair is completely disheveled, and I have a small hickey on my chest.

After a pleasant shower, I slip into fresh clothes and head for the kitchen. The smell of coffee quickly fills the room.

Holding the steaming mug in my hands, I look again at Emily, still asleep. Her eyes, her smile, her closeness - it all means so much more to me than I could ever put into words.

I also pour her a cup of the scalding black liquid and place it on the bedside table. Carefully, I lean over her and kiss her on the forehead.

"Emily... It's time to wake up," I whisper.

Her eyelids flutter and she finally opens her beautiful eyes. A sleepy smile forms on her lips, and I can't help but return it.

"Hello, sleepyhead," I say softly.

"Good morning," she murmurs, squirming in bed. "What a night..."

"Yes, huh..."

I hand her the cup of coffee and she accepts it gratefully.

"You're the best!" she says, taking a sip.

I just smile and sit on the edge of the bed. It's so familiar, so nice to be with her - even in these simple moments. But now it's time to face the challenges of the day. I have a training session to attend and Emily is starting her new job at the newspaper.

As she dresses, I can only stare at her, fascinated by her beauty.

"You look great," I whisper.

She smiles and winks at me.

"You're not bad yourself!" she argues, laughing.

I want to undress her straight away and spend the rest of

the day in bed with her. But instead, I force myself to hand her her bag.

The kiss she gives me is tender, before she turns away and heads for the road.

The day is now ahead of me, full of challenges and possibilities, and I feel that with Emily by my side, I can overcome anything.

The ice rink greets me with its familiar sounds - the scraping of skates and the clacking of sticks on the ice. But after training, something is different.

Chase and I are side by side, in full gear, waiting for Coach Franklyn. He says he wants to talk to us for a moment, and I can't help but stress.

It's not long before he approaches us and takes us both aside in his office. A smile spreads across his face, a sign, I hope, of good news. With each step, I feel my excitement rising.

"Have a seat, guys," he says, pointing to the chairs in front of his desk.

We take our seats, and he leans forward to stare at us with serious eyes.

"I wanted to tell you both personally that the scout present at the last game was extremely impressed by your performance."

I can hear my pulse pounding in my ears as I try to concentrate on his words. This information feels like a great victory. Chase and I look at each other, smiling broadly.

Coach Franklyn smiles.

"In fact, he was not only impressed by your sporting skills, but also by your academic records. Liam, you've done the right thing! He sees great potential in both of you. He firmly believes that you have what it takes to go far in the NHL."

Icebound Attraction

The words seem to hang in the air and I can hardly believe my luck. The NHL - it's every ice hockey player's dream! It's been mine since I was a kid! Chase also seems to need to digest what's just been said before reacting.

"He has already established contact with certain teams who are ready to come and observe you in upcoming games, and possibly draft you later."

We can hardly contain our joy. A feeling of gratitude and pride runs through me and I can't help but jump.

"It's crazy!" I exclaim.

Chase is just as enthusiastic.

"Dude! We made it!"

Coach Franklyn nods but keeps a straight face.

"Nothing's won yet, guys. You have the talent and the determination. Now it's up to you to work hard and seize the opportunity. The world of professional hockey is a challenge, but if you work hard enough, you can make it."

The coach's words penetrate deep into my consciousness. This chance is a gift and I'm ready to give it everything I've got.

Chase and I exchange a glance and I can see the same determination in his eyes.

"We're not going to fail, coach," I say, confident.

He smiles proudly.

"I know you won't. You've earned it."

He explains the details of the period ahead. And together, we leave the office with a sense of euphoria that's hard to put into words.

On the way to the locker room, I still can't believe my luck. I'm touching my dream with my fingertips! If I take this step, if I manage to show what I'm capable of during training sessions, and also during games, I have every chance of being taken in the draft, and so does Chase!

Icebound Attraction

And as I get rid of my gear, I feel that all the hardship, all the hard work and all the sacrifices were worth it.

Chase and I look at each other and we don't need words to know what the other is thinking. The future is ahead of us, and we're ready to seize it with both hands.

Completely fired up, we decide to celebrate and head for a bar we like, off campus.

The idea that this day could be the start of an exciting journey lends the atmosphere something magical. The bar is busy and the mood is festive. People are laughing, chatting and enjoying the moment. Chase and I look for a table and order some beers.

Each sip feels like a toast to the future, and the smiles on our faces are unwavering.

The euphoria lasts for a while until I remember that I haven't told Emily yet! Caught up in the joy of the moment, I completely forgot! Shame on me!

I quickly take my phone out of my pocket and send her a message. As I wait for her reply, the bar fills up more and more and the atmosphere becomes more cheerful.

It doesn't take long for my screen to light up, announcing a response.

* Liam, this is great! I'm so happy for you and Chase! Unfortunately, I've already made plans for tonight with the girls and I won't be able to join you to celebrate. But I'll raise my cup to your success!

Her words bring a smile to my face. Even if she can't be there, I know she's proud of me and that warms my heart.

I put down my phone and Chase toasts with me again. It promises to be an unforgettable night, and I'm determined to enjoy every minute of it. For once, we can give ourselves a little

Icebound Attraction

respite before getting right back into it!

Time flies and before you know it, it's midnight. The bar is still full, the music is blaring and the mood seems to have reached its peak. After a while, I notice a few women paying attention to us. Attempts to approach us are obvious. Interest is perceptible in their eyes. However, despite all the commotion around us, my thoughts turn to Emily. I gently decline their advances and turn back to my beer.

Chase looks at me and laughs.

"Brother, what's wrong with you?"

I smile.

"What's wrong with me? Can't I have a quiet party with my best friend?"

Chase nods and smiles in return.

"Yes, of course!" he replies.

An hour later, as we make our way back to campus, the city lights surround us in a soft glow. You'd think the night was endless. We stagger slowly, laughing over anecdotes.

"And remember when Mrs. Marshall forced us to clean up her yard?" exclaims Chase.

"Yes, I remember! Ugh! You decided to play with your father's leaf blower, and you got it absolutely everywhere!"

"You dared me to do it and I..."

Suddenly, out of the shadows.

"What the..."

Adrenalin rushes through my veins as I notice the glint of a screwdriver in the hand of the guy facing us.

"Give me your money, right now!" he growls.

Chase and I exchange a brief glance. We agree: surrendering without a fight is out of the question! We've been through so much already - we're not going to be intimidated by a thief, especially on our night of celebration. Besides, there are two of us, and we're both pretty hefty and younger than he is.

Unluckily, we forgot to take into account that we're completely drunk...

Without hesitation, we pounce on him, trying to wrest the screwdriver from his hands. But his resistance is more violent than expected and we find ourselves in a chaotic brawl.

Pain grips me as his fist lands in my stomach, but my resolve remains intact. Chase fights in his own way and we both try to stand up to our attacker. Clearly, we're dealing with a professional, and in a millisecond of inattention, he manages to wriggle free and knock us down one after the other with a powerful blow. My head hits the asphalt and I struggle to stay conscious.

The thief takes our wallets out of our jacket pockets and runs off.

What the hell?

Slowly, I get to my feet, staggering and staring angrily at his shadow around the corner.

As I fumble with my jacket to see what he's taken from me, I feel a liquid warming my belly. Anger turns to horror as I realize it's my blood. The screwdriver has hit my arm as well as my belly, but it seems to have rippled, and I've got a nasty gash running down to my hip. I'm also bleeding from my forehead, where I fell. The pain intensifies by the minute, and I swallow.

"Fucking asshole... Chase? Chase, are you okay?"

I turn to my best friend, still lying on the ground. He's breathing heavily, and his T-shirt is turning crimson where he's been hit.

"Shit! Chase!"

I throw myself on my knees beside him and he smiles at me with difficulty.

"We're really good at fighting, aren't we. If we tell this story, we'll have to turn it to our advantage!"

"How are you feeling?" I ask, worried to see him so pale.

"Well, I've been better... But I don't think it's that deep. It's mostly pain, really."

He tries to stand up and I talk him out of it.

My heart pounds in my ears as I reach for my cell phone and dial the emergency number. Luckily, I'd left it in my jeans pocket and our attacker hasn't stolen it!

The words pass my lips in a rush as I explain the situation.

It's not long before help arrives, followed by a police car, and the tension is replaced by a sense of relief.

As we describe the incident, I feel like I'm not really there. I'm sore, cold and clearly sobering up. Suddenly, the world seems a dangerous place and reality more brutal than ever.

The agents chat amongst themselves while an ambulance takes us away. Then we're driven to the nearest hospital with flashing lights and sirens blaring.

The pain from my screwdriver wounds is stinging, as I lie on the bunk of the vehicle. But I refuse to take anything to relieve the pain for fear of tarnishing my future blood tests. There's no way I'm going to be disqualified for this! I prefer to wait for the approval of the coach, whom I've informed by text. I don't care if it hurts! Chase is lying next to me, his face white.

Soon we arrive in the emergency department, and the nursing staff surround us.

The wounds caused by the screwdriver are not deep, thank God, but the pain is intense. My heartbeat echoes in my head.

The minutes stretch into hours, and the presence of the doctors and nurses reassure us. Franklyn ends up telling me to stop fooling around - basically - and take something to ease the pain. I'm grateful for that.

Chase and I are admitted for observation, because he has an ugly hole in his pectoral, and because of my blow to the head. They want to make sure I don't have a concussion. The monitor that indicates my heart rate is making high-pitched sounds, and that doesn't encourage me to calm down.

I can't help thinking how quickly everything can change. The path we've just taken seems tainted with uncertainty, and I'm beginning to think that all this could have a negative impact on future training sessions, game results and, by extension, our careers.

Holy shit!

As I lay pondering the events of the last few hours, hurried footsteps suddenly echo down the corridor and voices murmur with apprehension. The door to my hospital room opens on Emily, followed by Coach Franklyn.

My heartbeat quickens when I see her, and all my pain seems to fade into the background for a moment. Her face is marked by concern, and I can see the determination in her eyes. Her presence is like a light in the darkness, giving me hope.

"Em!" I exclaim, my voice hoarse.

Without hesitation, she rushes towards me. Tears glisten in her eyes. Her embrace is so warm and comforting that I forget for a moment where I am and what has happened. It's as if the world around us disappears and only the two of us exist.

"I came as quickly as I could after your text. I was so scared for you!" she mutters, hugging me tightly.

I return her embrace; with all the strength I can muster.

"I'm fine. We're both fine."

The coach stands next to us, his gaze shifting from Chase to me.

"You're both idiots!" he says, shaking his head. "But I'm glad you're safe and alive!"

Chase, lying in bed, smiles.

"We resisted, coach!" he croaks.

Emily detaches herself from me and walks over to him. She

puts a hand on his shoulder and gives him an encouraging smile.

"And that's where it got you..." she sighs.

We tell them briefly what happened, and the atmosphere relaxes a little.

She comes back to me and sits on the edge of the bed. Her hand finds mine and her warmth spreads throughout my body. It feels good to know that I have her support.

"I thought my heart would stop when I got your message," she says softly, her eyes fixed on mine.

"I'm fine," I repeat. "The wounds aren't deep; they're just keeping us under observation. But I'm... I'm glad you're here."

I kiss her hand and she smiles softly.

We're brought back to reality by Chase's throat clearing.

Stunned, we raise our eyes together, looking in turn at the witnesses to our exchange.

Caught up in the joy of our reunion, we completely forgot about Chase and Coach Franklyn.

Shit...

13

Emily

I look at Chase and when our eyes meet, reality hits me like a punch.

Shit, I completely forgot about him and the coach!

Tense, I look at the coach, who doesn't flinch and still stares at us, arms folded. Chase, meanwhile, smiles at us, and the mischief in his eyes doesn't go unnoticed.

Heat rises to my cheeks, and I turn to Liam. He in turn clears his throat and searches for the right words.

"Yes, well... Er..." he starts to justify himself.

Chase raises a hand to interrupt.

"It's okay, Liam. I've known for a while. And I'm happy for you both."

He smiles warmly.

I'm breathing a little easier. The fact that Chase is reacting positively means a lot to me. I know he's a very important person in Liam's life, so I was hoping he wouldn't take it the wrong way.

Coach Franklyn's voice rings out from a corner of the room: "That explains a lot..."

The tension immediately returns and Liam's grip on my hand strengthens too.

"Liam, I've told you more than once that this kind of thing distracts you from what's important."

He stares at Liam before continuing.

"But it seems to me to be more than just a distraction..."

A slight smile appears on his face.

"You both gave me a huge scare and I... I'm glad you have someone who cares about you so much. It's a precious thing," he finally says.

I can't believe what I'm hearing. I look at Coach Franklyn in amazement.

Are those tears shining in his eyes?

A nurse chooses this moment to enter the room, and she allows us to focus on something else. She checks the monitors and turns to us.

"Visiting hours are over. I'm sorry, but you have to leave now."

It's with some reluctance that I say goodbye to the boys. I'd rather spend the night by Liam's side. He smiles faintly and I can see both fatigue and disappointment in his eyes.

I take his hand in mine and squeeze gently.

"I'll be back tomorrow, as soon as I can. I promise."

He smiles wearily and his hand grips mine tighter.

"Thanks, Em. I'm sorry I scared you..."

Before leaving, I lean in once more and kiss him tenderly. Now that Chase and the coach know, I don't want to miss out!

"See you tomorrow, get some rest," I say, shaking my hand.

On the way to campus, I feel a little empty. Even though I know Liam is in good hands and out of danger, I'm worried.

I can't shake the idea that I could have lost him tonight, right there, all of a sudden, as quickly as the blink of an eye. This fear has lodged itself inside me, and I realize how important he has become in my life.

I rub my hands together nervously.

The positive thing to come out of all this is that both Chase and the coach now know. That takes some of the weight off our secret. And they reacted well! I know it was important for Liam not to disappoint his coach, and I'm glad he didn't yell at us and say it was a big mistake.

No sooner have I reached my bedroom door than I pull out my cell phone and dial Maddie's number. I need someone I can tell all this to. When she picks up, the words pour out of my mouth and I tearfully explain the whole situation - my relationship with Liam, the attack, his injuries, my fear, everything...

Maddie's voice is reassuring when she answers.

"Oh, my darling! Thank God the boys are okay. You'll be fine, do you want me to come?"

"I'm fine, I was just very, very scared..." I reply.

"I understand, yes. And thank you for finally telling me about your relationship, it took a while, but I'm glad you did."

I open my mouth and close it again. I pick myself up and move on:

"You... you suspected?"

She laughs.

"Of course! After what you told me last time about you and Liam, about your feelings for him, and all the nights you'd supposedly 'fallen asleep at the newspaper's office', even though I was the last one to close the door, or that you had 'something planned' and couldn't join Cassy and me, yeah I suspected!"

I blush.

"I'm sorry... I shouldn't have kept it from you."

"Emily, I've told you before, just because we're best friends doesn't mean you have to tell me everything. You needed time, so I don't mind. And I also assume you didn't want anyone to know."

"Yes... Thank you, Maddie... Thank you, really."

I feel tears welling up in the corners of my eyes.

Feeling grateful and much calmer, I hang up the phone and drop onto my bed.

★★★

The next day, a mixture of nervousness and anticipation accompanies me on my way to the hospital. I want to make sure they're feeling better and let them know I'm there if they need anything.

When I knock on the door of the hospital room and walk in, I'm greeted by an impressive array of flowers, stuffed animals and gifts. The room exudes color and warmth, and I can't help but laugh. Apparently, a lot of people have heard about the incident and want to show their support.

I glance at one of the cards tied around a teddy bear holding a heart in its paws, and let out a grunt when I read that it's from one of Liam's admirers.

Yeah... I should have known!

An unfamiliar man sits between the two beds, chatting with Liam and Chase. He exudes authority.

When I enter, he ends the conversation and turns to me.

"I'll be back to see you at the next game," he says, before standing up and nodding in my direction.

Is this the agent Liam told me about?

I smile at him shyly and take a step back so as not to disturb him on his way to the door.

Once he's out, I go and check on the wounded. I greet Chase and kiss Liam, who gives me a beautiful smile.

"So, how are you feeling today?"

"Better, now that you're here!" laughs Liam.

Chase nods in agreement.

"I'm not happy to see you for the same reasons, but thanks

for coming, Emily. It's so boring here!"

"And yet you have plenty of little notes to read," I slip in mischievously.

Liam and Chase laugh.

"It's crazy... I didn't think we'd get so many. We're getting out soon and yet it makes the whole campus think we're dead!"

Liam tightens his grip on my hand and his eyes suddenly sparkle.

"By the way, that recruiter I told you about, Mr. Turner, just stepped out."

My gaze moves to the door.

"Looks like you both impressed him enough to make the trip in person!"

Chase smiles.

"Well, he's predicted a pretty good future for us. Which is very reassuring, given that we're likely to be a little slow in the first few training sessions. But we'll be back on our feet in no time."

Liam nods in agreement and I can see the determination in their eyes. The dream they're chasing is more tangible than ever, and I'm sure they'll do anything to make it come true.

Time flies with them and I suddenly realize it's time to go. I have to get back to the *New York Post* and I can't afford to be late.

Tingles of excitement run through my belly. It's a demanding schedule, between my classes, newspaper work, the internship and my relationship with Liam, but it's worth every minute. Right from the start of my internship, I've been given interesting topics to write about in short articles. And so far, the feedback on my work has been positive. Only the hectic pace of the writing process is giving me a bit of a hard time. I feel like I'm constantly working against the clock, because the deadlines for getting everything done are pretty tight over there.

I say goodbye, give my sexy boyfriend a kiss and hurriedly gather my things.

When I leave the hospital and head for the *New York Post*, I slip into the shoes of Emily the journalist, and push aside the feelings that twist my heart when I leave Liam.

I arrive just in time at the newspaper and my supervisor approaches me at a brisk pace.

"Ready for another hard day's work, Emily?" he asks with a straight face.

I swallow.

"Yes, Mr. Roberts, I'm more than ready."

"Well, I've got a research assignment for you."

I'm hoping it'll distract me a bit, and already he's handing me a stack of documents.

"There's an important event next week, and I need thorough research on the guest speaker. I expect a detailed report from you by the end of the day."

I nod and grab the documents.

As I sit down at my desk, my thoughts gradually drift away from the events of the last twenty-four hours. The task ahead demands my full concentration, and I have no room for error.

As the day draws to a close, I finally gather enough material to write my summary. I sit down at my computer and start sorting through the relevant facts. As I write, a certain sense of accomplishment spreads through me. The work soothes me and helps me put my thoughts in order. It's as if I've found a peaceful island in the middle of a storm. Once I've finished my essay, I hand it in to my supervisor and gather my things to go home.

On the way, I take stock of my day. It's not easy to juggle personal concerns and professional responsibilities. And in the midst of all these challenges, I also have to pay attention to my own needs and those of the people around me.

I sigh.

So, this is what it means to become an adult?

The exhaustion of recent events begins to show as I cross the threshold into my bedroom. Taking advantage of Cassy's absence, I drop onto the sofa and close my eyes for a moment.

After staying like that for a few minutes, I sit up and take out my cell phone. I text Liam to explain that I won't be able to come to the hospital tomorrow. It's costing me, but I need time to concentrate on my university homework, which has fallen behind with my internship. Going back and forth from the campus to the hospital takes time, and it won't help me... On top of that, I have to admit I'm exhausted.

I hope he'll understand, even if the idea of not seeing him doesn't appeal to me at all.

14

Emily

I enter the classroom building with a bittersweet feeling. I've spent half the night working on homework and preparing for an exam. So I'm tired, and on top of that, grumpy.

As I cross the corridor, my eye is caught by a large poster on the wall. It looks like the *End-of-spring Gala is* only two weeks away. Already... the academic year has flown by!

The idea of an evening of fun and dancing seems both seductive and remote to me at this moment. Still, it's very tempting to go.

I lean against the wall and stare at the colorful image.

University galas are events I've studiously avoided. I didn't have the heart to go with Cassy and Maddie. They're more like couples' nights, and I was sure I'd be a good sport. But this time, I feel different. I'm in a relationship that, although 'secret', is important. In a way, I want to show the rest of the campus how happy I am. And maybe it's time we tell the truth about Liam and me as a couple...

I miss him, and not seeing him today gives me a little twinge of sadness.

As I enter the amphitheater, a mixture of anticipation and uncertainty spreads through me. A message from Liam pulls me out of my reflections and brings my first smile of the day.

Hi there! Guess what? I'm can leave the hospital today! Can we meet at the end of the day? I have something to tell you! <3

I'm relieved to hear that he's doing better and can't wait to see him, and I'm also curious about this thing he wants to tell me about. But I still have work to do. I tell him I'll drop by later this afternoon, can't wait to see him, and get back to concentrating on the course.

Later, when I go to the campus newspaper to pick up the list of articles I have to write, the editor seems to be waiting for me.

"Hey, Emily!"

"Hi David," I greet him, surprised that he'd come to talk to me, as he's usually overworked and pays little attention to his subordinates.

Let's not forget that I'm still a first-year!

"How's your internship at the *New York Post* going?"

"Uh, great... Thank you..."

"It's really exceptional for a first-year to be selected to work there. I hope you realize how lucky you are!" he exclaims, his mouth pursed, as if vexed at not having been chosen.

Man, it's not my fault I got the job...

"I saw that they had published the list of players possibly drafted for the NHL."

My heart misses a beat.

I've been so busy today, I haven't even glanced at today's publication, and I didn't know the list was coming out now! I can't wait to find out if a particular name is on it... Suddenly, apprehension knots my stomach as if it were my own future.

"Ha?" I feign, my surprise for the moment being genuine.

"Yes, and two members of our university team seem to be

in a good position. That's great!"

My mouth goes dry.

"I want you to write an article about them."

"And who is it?" I ask, putting an end to this unbearable suspense.

"Chase Carter and Liam Scott. Both are promising talents, and our readers would certainly be interested to know more. I'm sure you're familiar with them, having covered every hockey game since the start of the season."

Now my heart is racing and I'm nodding, trying to look calm.

"It's a great idea!"

"Of course, I'd like you to go a little further in your research..."

I frown.

"What do you mean 'further'?"

"Find something that attracts attention, surprises and captivates."

Faced with my silence and refusal to understand, he adds with a sigh:

"A scandal, Emily!"

Shock overwhelms me.

The idea of looking for scandalous details about Chase and Liam seems disgusting to me. Yes, I'm a journalist and my job is to find interesting stories, but I'm also bound by certain principles. Interesting doesn't mean it has to be juicy gossips!

"I understand that you're looking for a compelling story," I begin, taking a step back. "But I don't think the emphasis on sensationalism serves the paper. It should be about their success and performance, not potential scandals."

David sighs, looking annoyed.

"Emily, you want to be a journalist, don't you? That includes getting your hands a little dirty. A little controversy will make the paper more appealing."

I can understand his point of view, but do I have to betray my principles?

"I can always put someone else on it, but inevitably, if it reaches the ears of the *New York Post* that you're already being picky about the subjects you're given for our university paper...."

He stretches out a knowing smile.

This guy is an asshole!

My work here will inevitably be reflected in my academic record, and if he gives me a bad grade, that's it for me!

All of a sudden, I feel lost and can't think straight. I can't dig up scandals about Liam and Chase. That would be... horrible! On the other hand, being a journalist is everything I've ever dreamed of and the campus newspaper is an important, if not mandatory, step in my career.

I close my eyes and breathe deeply.

I reluctantly nod and leave the office with mixed feelings.

Journalists, as I have learned, have a responsibility to ensure balanced and ethically defensible coverage. Up to now, I've always respected this principle. But now...

As I return to my room, I reflect on the balance between my personal convictions and the demands of my profession. Generally speaking, the line between interesting reporting and sensational journalism is often blurred. But I'd hoped I'd never find myself in such a situation and have to reconsider my convictions. Besides, this is the man I love and his best friend we're talking about, which makes the situation even more complicated.

Eventually, we get to this problem of bias! What will people think of my journalistic integrity when they find out I'm sleeping with Liam Scott?

I sit down at my desk and stare at my laptop screen.

There must be some way to satisfy David without jeopardizing my personal relationships or my career.

Maybe I should start with Chase; we haven't been friends for long. My relationship with Liam is much more complicated. And maybe I won't find anything scandalous after all!

A simple Internet search won't do, so I'm going to start with social networks. There's always a lot of information out there. I'm always surprised to see how much people reveal about themselves. After that, I might also interview a few members of the team.

The afternoon passes quickly and suddenly I realize what time it is. I hurry to gather my things. I promised Liam I'd come and see him at the end of the day.

I completely overlooked the fact that he was on the draft list, and I guess he wanted to talk to me about it tonight.

When I stand in front of his room and knock, the door opens with lightning speed. Liam stands in front of me with a big smile on his face.

"Em!" he exclaims excitedly, hugging me tightly.

I realize how much I've missed him when I snuggle up to him and breathe in his scent. His arms are a familiar place where I feel good. But tonight is different - excitement dances in Liam's eyes.

"There's something I need to tell you," he begins, euphoric, unable to conceal his enthusiasm.

I smile inwardly.

He's so cute when he's excited.

He imitates a drum roll before continuing.

"I made it! I'm on the list of young hopefuls for the draft! And so is Chase! That's fantastic!"

A smile spreads across my face as I try to look surprised. I don't want to spoil his joy by telling him I already know.

"That's amazing, Liam! Congratulations!"

I hug him and kiss him hungrily. His face lights up with pride and his eyes sparkle.

"I can hardly believe it. Well, it's not over yet! The next few games will be decisive for the standings, but Mr. Turner has assured us that he'll be bringing in teams who might be interested in our recruitment, to come and watch us play. It's a great opportunity, and it means we've still got a good chance of going pro!"

I take his face in my hands.

"I'm so proud of you. You've worked hard and you've really earned it!"

Liam just smiles and kisses me effusively. We talk for a while about his plans and upcoming games. Then I decide to turn the conversation to another subject.

"By the way, the *End-of-Spring Gala* is coming up," I say innocently.

"I've heard yes! Are you planning to go?" he asks, like I'm talking about the weather.

Slowly, I nod and consider how best to phrase the next question.

"Would you... er... well, maybe... consider going together? As a *couple*, I mean?"

His eyes narrow slightly.

"Ha... It's... an important decision..."

His reluctance is palpable.

"I... I understand your concern. But I think this could be a special moment and take the pressure off us to hide our relationship from everyone."

I look into his eyes.

"Besides, Coach Franklyn already knows, and he's the one you were worried about," I conclude.

He sighs and strokes his growing beard.

"Yes. It's just... there are so many things I have to think

about. My career, how the public will react...."

I put my hand on his.

"I'm not asking you to give me an answer right away. Just think it over calmly."

A smile passes over his face, and he shakes my hand.

"You're the best, Em."

I wrap my arms around him, and rest my head in the hollow of his neck.

Suddenly, I feel him take a breath.

"Let's go to the gala together," he says in a deep voice. "If you're ready, I'm ready."

★★★

It's finally the weekend, and I'm relieved to have a break from work. It's time to get ready for the gala, and I've been looking forward to it for days.

Maddie and Cassy are also going and we agreed to go last-minute shopping, as they were unsure of their outfits, and I haven't had time to buy one yet. So far, every day has been packed to the brim.

As we rummage through the racks, I'm overwhelmed by the multitude of options. Sparkling evening gowns and elegant gala dresses hang everywhere and seem to compete with each other.

We spend hours trying on different clothes, chatting and exchanging opinions.

Cassy observes me as I look at a particularly showy dress.

"Emily, this is the one for you!"

I laugh and shake my head.

"I think it might be a little too sexy for my taste."

Maddie approaches me and looks at the dress critically.

"You're right, maybe it is a little too... hot."

She winks at me and wiggles her eyebrows knowingly.

She's right. The dress is daring, but it would make me look my best. And the gala is the best opportunity to think outside the box!

Back in our student room, I sit on my bed and brood.

So far, my research into Liam and Chase hasn't turned up anything that would satisfy David. Even interviews with team members haven't turned up much. Nobody has anything negative to say about them. But damn it! I've got to find a solution if I don't want to get fucked over by the other moron. Of course, I could explain my position to the *New York Post* if they found out, but they'd think I was a pain in the ass and, after my internship, they'd drop me from their list of open positions altogether. I'm well aware of how the business works, and when you're seen as being too demanding, they prefer not to follow through.

I shake my head.

I shouldn't worry about that now, because tonight we're dancing. And with Liam! Probably under the curious eyes of the whole university too! David's the one who's going to feel his jaw drop...

I don't know if I'm right to do it, but maybe it'll also help me get out of this mess. Maybe he'll decide I shouldn't pursue my research if he knows I'm likely to tell Liam?

Cassy snaps me out of my thoughts by nagging me to get ready. Maddie then joins us and we help each other finalize our outfits.

When I look in the mirror, I have to admit I'm pretty proud of my look. A floor-length red dress molds my body perfectly, with a side slit that highlights my legs. I wear it with red lipstick and a high braid with a red silk ribbon.

A little more bust and I could have looked like Jessica

Icebound Attraction

Rabbit[6]!

Cassy and Maddie are gorgeous. In her short sequined dress, Cassy is as cheerful and radiant as ever. As for Maddie, she opted for a classic look: a short black dress, high heels and loose hair.

I look at them, proud and happy to have such good friends with me. This evening can only be exceptional!

A moment later, they're picked up by their respective dates, while I'm still waiting for Liam.

I look nervously at my watch and head for the bathroom for the fourth time to check my eyeliner. He's late... and I'm beginning to wonder if he's changed his mind.

In the end, maybe it wasn't such a good idea to suggest that we make our relationship public. Maybe he's...

A knock on the door jolts me out of my dark thoughts.

Relieved and excited at the same time, I rush to the door. Liam is there, in a breathtaking suit. His eyes sparkle and his brown curls fall seductively over his face. He whistles with approval when he sees me and blows me a kiss on the cheek so as not to ruin my lipstick.

"You're stunning, Em!"

"You too!"

Right away, all I want to do is take off his clothes and find out what's underneath. But I decide to be reasonable and keep the urges in check. However, as I approach him to leave the room, he holds my hand and presses me against the door.

Slowly, I feel his warm hand move up the slit of my dress to nestle between my boiling thighs.

"Not so fast," he murmurs against my mouth, still careful not to smudge my make-up.

I feel my body catch fire, and soon one of his fingers slips

---

6 Jessica Rabbit is a fictional character created for the film *Who Framed Roger Rabbit* (1988).

past the edge of my lingerie to titillate me.

I groan, arching against him to encourage him.

"You're hot, Em..."

And with his other hand, he guides me to the bulge in his pants, turning me on.

His index finger makes circles on my pleasure-swollen intimacy, and I start to pant. Slowly, he inserts himself inside me, as if testing my desire.

"You're so wet..."

His husky voice transports me, and I beg him to continue.

Unable to take it any longer, he penetrates me with a second finger and sends me soaring into the clouds. I come hard against the door, unable to hold back a scream.

Satisfied, he withdraws, licks his fingers greedily, his gaze incandescent with lust, and suddenly turns me around.

I can hear him undoing his pants, grabbing a condom, as he lifts my dress over my butt and pulls down my panties. With my hands flat against the wood, I push my hips towards him, impatient. Soon, I feel his hot dick at the entrance to my intimacy. He rubs himself against me, lubricating himself with my pleasure before penetrating me with force. There, he takes me without warning, giving his all. After only a few minutes, our excitement is so obvious, we climax at the same moment.

"Fuck... you got me too excited..." he almost apologizes. "But I didn't want to risk ruining your beauty routine!"

We laugh and adjust our clothes, our cheeks flushed with shared pleasure.

Finally, we set off, more united than ever after this exquisite moment of sex.

With every step we take towards the gala, I get a little more nervous. I wonder how everyone will react when they find out we're here. *And together.*

"Are you ready?" Liam asks before we enter the room, stroking my back.

I nod nervously and we push open the heavy doors.

15

The gala room opens up before us and the music blares as Emily and I enter arm in arm. It's a wonderful feeling to no longer have to hide my affection for her. Our torrid embrace has literally galvanized me and I feel ready to take on the world.

The twinkling lights and the cheerful murmur of the students present create a pleasant atmosphere. The ambiance is chic yet relaxed. Rhythmic music vibrates through the speakers without being deafening.

We cross the room to join our friends we've spotted near the bar, and behind us a few heads turn. Still, we're a long way from the big buzz we thought we'd generate by showing up together. *Phew!*

As I order us something to drink, I notice out of the corner of my eye an all-too-familiar curly redhead - what the hell! One of my ex-girlfriends glares at us and my heart rate quickens, but I decide to ignore her.

We grab our drinks and hang around the counter to enjoy the atmosphere. Our friends, who seem to like each other, are out on the dance floor, doing their best choreography.

I really need to tell Chase he can't dance...

I can't help laughing as I watch him do it, and soon Emily

joins them.

Suddenly, I feel a presence beside me, and I excuse myself by pushing back my stool to make room. A throat-clearance pulls me from my observation and I look up at the person in question.

An uneasy feeling overcomes me when our eyes meet.

My ex again...

The expression on her face is hard to interpret - a mixture of surprise and maybe also displeasure. I can't deny that she and I didn't part on the friendliest of terms. Still, water has passed under the bridge, and I hope she'll get off my back. I don't need that tonight. I just want to enjoy Emily and my friends.

"Liam, hi," she finally says, smiling falsely.

"Sara," I answer soberly.

"I've heard that you have a chance of being drafted, congrats!" she continues.

I nod and we talk for a few more minutes before I feel it's time to end the conversation. I don't think it's right to talk to one of my exes on my first date with my official girlfriend. It also has to be said that Sara has never been the best date in the world. And I don't want to be associated with her. Campus rumors are rife, and already my arrival with Emily has aroused a bit of curiosity, so I'd like to avoid a scandal along the lines of 'Liam Scott was seen with his ex again at the End of Spring Gala, where he also introduced of his new girlfriend'.

"I'll leave you to it and go dancing with my friends."

I don't have the nerve to say that this meeting was a pleasure, and Sara nods before looking towards the group.

"Sure... Have fun, Liam."

I take my leave politely and head for Emily.

As we dance, laugh and enjoy our evening, I always feel a gaze upon me. And every time I turn my head in the direction of the bar, I see my ex staring bitterly at us.

She's gonna be all over you, man...

Sara took our separation very hard. But I couldn't cope with her addiction problems. As an avid sportsman who wanted to become a professional, she wasn't helping me. I tried to reach out to her, but every time I did, she turned to drugs. I picked her up several times in a bad way, and one day that was the last straw. But that's all in the past, and I'd hoped that running into her again wouldn't arouse so much anger on her part.

As Emily and I head back to the bar for a breather, Sara approaches us with a determined step.

What the hell is she up to?

"So, you're the 'new girl'?" she asks, mimicking quotation marks with her fingers.

Emily pauses in surprise and turns her eyes to me for a moment before returning to Sara.

"Uh, the new what?" she says, as if trying to understand what my ex is referring to.

"What did he say to get you? That you were important? That he wanted you in his life? He probably fucked you pretty hard, huh? It's a good fuck, you've got to admit."

Emily opens her mouth in shock as I try to come between them. Sara seems to have had a few too many drinks while I was dancing, and her breath is now quite heavy.

That, and the coke she must have snorted in the bathroom...

"You'd better shut up, Sara. And get yourself a glass of water. You're in no condition now," I growl menacingly.

"Or what? People might find out that you got high with me once or twice?"

My eyes widen.

I would never touch that shit!

All around us, people are starting to gather to find out what's going on. Inevitably, you always attract vultures in this kind of situation.

"What did he say? Did he fuck you before or after he told you he loved you? For me, it was before. Liam's not exactly known for keeping his dick in his pants!"

I blush. It could not get any worse!

"In fact, as soon as he dumped me, he was banging one of the cheerleaders in the rink's locker room. Who knows if he wasn't already sleeping with her when we were together. He's like that... pretty sexually hyperactive! In fact, I don't know how long you've been together, but not so long ago, he was banging the yoga teacher..."

Well, it could be worse...

Suddenly, Chase bursts in between us and grabs Sara by the arm, pulling her back.

"Get lost..." he intimates, raising his eyebrows and giving her a sufficiently convincing look.

"That's it, the cavalry's coming! The bisexual on duty is your knight in shining armor again!"

My best friend doesn't loosen his grip and carries Sara, who is still screaming horrors, out of the room.

The students present have not missed a beat, and I can see some of them filming with their phones.

I'm overcome with disgust and turn to the livid Emily, who hasn't moved a millimeter.

"I... Em..."

"It's okay, Liam. Don't say anything," she says, her voice trembling.

She smoothes her dress with the flat of her hand, and without another word leaves the gala. I follow her with bewildered eyes, wondering whether to chase after her or let her digest the whole thing.

Icebound Attraction

My anger at my ex bubbles up inside me, I'm also mad at myself, because I should have known what was going to happen. Sara has always been a pain in the ass, and this was too good an opportunity for revenge.

When Chase returns, he puts my hand on my shoulder, pulling me out of my dark thoughts.

"What's up, man?"

"I should be asking you that. Fuck, I'm sorry, bro."

"Oh, don't worry, my bisexuality's no secret, and I don't mind being flaunted," he replies with a smile. "On the other hand, the other slut didn't miss you. Where's Emily?"

He looks around, puzzled.

"She's gone..."

"Rha shit... Is she mad?"

"I guess so. When the other person's past jumps in your face and throws horrors at you, I think you're entitled to be. Or at least, she must be hurt..." I sigh.

"She'll soon see through this bullshit. She knows you, Liam, and she loves you."

"We've never said it before..."

"That you love each other?" asks my best friend in surprise.

"Not officially, not in person," I explain, scratching the back of my neck.

"What the fuck are you waiting for, man? For another Sara to beat the shit out of you in public? You know you're opening yourself up to a pro career, and there'll be dozens of chicks like that. And just for the fun of it, they'll come and ruin your life and relationship, because you'll be more famous than ever. If you don't do it..."

I nod. He's so right.

Right now, all I want is to get out of here. Get out and calm my mind. I'll talk to Emily, yes, but I'll let her digest this. I know she won't respond to my messages anyway, and there's no point in joining her in her room. Incidentally, I notice that Cassy and Maddie have left, and I assume they must be cheering her up.

I struggle with my feelings. Anger, worry, confusion - they all collide inside me. The next few weeks are going to be exhausting. The training sessions will come and go and I'll hardly have time to see Emily, let alone if she refuses to talk to me. It's frustrating.

I sigh and rub my face.

I hope we can settle this quickly. I hate being left with misunderstandings. And this girl is under my skin...

★★★

The next morning, I get up early. Chase and I have an intensive training session today to prepare for the upcoming games, and for the scouts who will be coming to observe us.

When we're on the ice, I focus on hockey and my thoughts take a back seat. The cold of the rink beneath my skates, the sound of the air whistling in my ears, the clash of the puck - everything feels familiar and in its rightful place.

Our movements are synchronized, our passes are precise, our shots are powerful. It's still an incredible feeling. The tension of the previous weeks dissipates for a moment. The sweat beads on my forehead, my muscles are working hard, and that gives me a certain satisfaction.

After the workout, I feel exhausted, but in a good way. I decide to text Emily to see if she's okay. The silence between us gnaws at me.

But... no reaction.

I'm about to give up hope when her answer arrives.

* *I need time.*

* *Let me at least explain, Em. You don't have my side of the story!*

* *Not yet, Liam.*

* *Don't be fooled by what that girl said. Nothing was true!*

* *Oh, I think there was a bit of truth, and it hurts. Of course, I knew that you'd had relations before*
me, but it's always funny when someone spits it in your face in such a crude way. That and
other things, she said... Anyway. Give me time.

I let out a sigh. It's understandable that she needs to think about all this, but also unfair. She didn't get my side of the story!
I wish I could reassure her, hold her close to me, and tell her that I simply love her.

★★★

I sit down in front of my computer, tense, to consult the results of my latest exams. My fingers tremble slightly, which is rather unheard of considering how little interest I had in my studies before.
Fuck, I did it!
The grades are unanimous, and I feel a new joy welling up inside me. It feels good to know that at least something in my life isn't going wrong!
It's all thanks to the hours I spent with Emily at the library when she patiently took the time to explain to me how to study better. Now, at least, I can see the fruits of all her efforts.

A bittersweet smile spreads across my face and I take a deep breath.

You're on the right track, Liam.

With every new challenge in training and every successful exam, I feel I'm growing - both as a hockey player and as a person. I just wish I could share it with her...

I hope Emily realizes how much I'm working on myself, not just in my career or studies, but in our relationship as well. I want to prove to her that I'm a good man, that I care about her. Now she just has to accept seeing me.

As I check my cell phone with the urge to send Emily a message, I receive several notifications that suddenly darken my mood.

What the hell?

Several students have shared an article from the campus newspaper, tagging me. My heart suddenly starts beating faster when I read the subject in question.

The title alone gives me a shock.

'A ROCKY ROAD TO THE NHL: LIAM SCOTT'S DARK PAST REVEALED.'

I can't believe it! The article not only contains details about my childhood that I'd never made public, but also shocking statements about my past, about my exes, especially Sara. It's suggested that I've been in contact with drug addicts, that I've used drugs myself and even that I have been dealing!

It's completely crazy!

Anger wells up inside me. How can someone spread such lies? How can someone manipulate my past and slander me like that? I feel betrayed, as if my story has been stolen and distorted.

And then I see the author's name. Everything stops. I can

feel the bile rising in my mouth. I want to throw up.

Emily Hansen.

I can't believe she's behind this rag. No, not her! There must be some explanation for all this. She can't be that mad at me for having ex-girlfriends, she can't be that mad at me for what Sara said when she was completely stoned, she can't blame me for the scene she made, damn it, to the point of jeopardizing my future! Especially since she was full of shit! And I never had a chance to explain myself, to tell her what was going on!

She, whom I believed to be honest and upright, has written an article exposing horrible lies. It's just insane!

My hands clench as I reread her writings. The words burn into my brain, and I feel helpless and hurt.

Why did Emily do this? Did she not trust me and our relationship enough? Did she want revenge? No... This is so unlike her...

I need to get some fresh air and try to sort out my emotions, which are spiraling in my head.

I make my way to the campus bar where Chase works. I can feel the stares coming my way, and this time they're not appreciative like the last few articles extolling my virtues.

Chase greets me with a smile, but quickly loses interest when he sees my face.

"What's going on, man? You seen a ghost?"

I hand him my phone so he can read the article. I can see the same shock on his face. His eyes scan the lines, and I can see the moment when his thoughts take the same direction as mine.

"Fuck, Liam... This sucks. It really does."

I just nod silently, unable to find the words to express what's going on inside me.

"No but wait. She couldn't write that. Not Emily! Did you

call her?"

I shake my head negatively.

"I'd rather calm down first," I say.

Chase nods in understanding.

"I understand, yes. Would you like a drink?"

"No, it's a bit early for that, and we've got practice later, so thank you, Brother. I'm gonna go home and crash for a while. I need to think."

"Take care of yourself and let me know if you learn anything."

I greet my best friend, and return to my room, my heart heavy.

I need to be alone to sort out my ideas, to know how to deal with all this, and above all what impact it might have on my career.

Coach Franklyn is going to have a fit too...

Finally, I reach for my cell phone and dial Mr. Turner's number.

He has years of experience in the world of professional ice hockey, and this certainly isn't the first shit he's had to deal with. I need his advice, and I think I can trust him.

When he takes the call, I try to keep my voice calm and measured, even if my thoughts are racing.

"Liam! How's it going? Training going well?" he asks, picking up the phone.

"Things are going well on that front, yes. But I was calling you about something else..."

I tell him the problem and he listens attentively.

"Liam, I understand your concern. But you should know that this kind of article is unfortunately part of your new reality. Especially if you get in the NHL. Journalists, even university journalists, are always on the lookout for sordid stories, and sometimes they cross the line. Don't let it get you down."

His words reassure me a little, but the uncertainty persists.
"But this article is a pack of lies!"
He sighs.
"Unfortunately, it happens more often than you might think. The public loves scandal, and some journalists will do anything to get attention. You have to learn to deal with it and concentrate on what's important: your performance on the ice. The best thing is not to read this kind of crap."
Tired, I rub my face.
"Do you think this article could influence my chances of being drafted?" I ask, unsure.
His voice is firm when he answers.
"No, Liam. It's your performance on the ice that's judged, not what you do with your private life, whether it's true or not. What the teams are interested in is your ability as a player and your professionalism. Don't let things like that affect you."
I breathe deeply as his words slowly percolate through me.
"Thank you, Mr. Turner."
"No problem, Liam. If you have any questions or need support, I'm always here. Just keep doing what you do best: playing. The rest, you don't care about."
After hanging up, I feel a little more relieved. His words bring me comfort and help me see the light at the end of the tunnel.
Come on, man, hold on!

When it's time to train, I feel a bit better. On the ice, I can put my thoughts aside for a while and concentrate on the sport. A temporary relief.
When I arrive at the rink, my eyes are immediately drawn to a mass of blond hair sitting in the stands.
A twinge runs through my heart.
Emily...

Chase notices my gaze and follows. Without hesitation, he moves towards her before I can stop him, and I watch helplessly as he strikes up a conversation with her.

What the hell is he telling her?

A few minutes later, which seems like an eternity, she gathers her things and leaves without even looking at me. What little hope I had of explaining ourselves leaves with her, and I wonder more and more whether she wrote the damn article or not.

When Chase comes back to me, the lump in my throat seems to have grown out of proportion. Still, I need to know.

"What did you say to her?" I ask point-blank.

He sighs.

"I told her she wasn't welcome here at the moment. She seemed very uncomfortable and tried to explain several times. But we're about to train, and we need to focus. If you need to talk, make an appointment, but don't do it on a stretch of bench between two practices. If you're upset, it'll upset the whole team, you know that."

I lower my eyes to the ice.

"You're right, man. We're acting like a couple of kids. She can't avoid me anymore, or at least doesn't want to. But for all that, she hasn't tried to call me or sent me any messages."

"So, you know what you have to do when you get out of here," Chase replies.

I thank him for looking after me and getting my head straight. Turner told me too: nothing must interfere with my goals when I'm training. And Emily is unfortunately one of those disruptions.

He puts a comforting hand on my shoulder.

"It won't be easy, but you have to get through it," he adds more gently. "And now, focus!"

Together, we take to the ice. I feel the energy and concentration gradually returning to me with each skate.

The other team members join us, and they all have the decency not to talk about the article. I guess Chase must have told them to keep their mouths shut, because even the most talkative ones don't say anything. I'm relieved and give it my all. A pleasant warmth spreads through my muscles and I focus on every step, every movement.

Training lasts two hours and the intensity doesn't let up for a second. By the time it's over, I'm totally exhausted. We've worked hard together, and this also strengthens our team spirit.

As I leave the rink, I can feel the tiredness in my limbs, but also the confidence in my ability to fight. It's a confidence I haven't felt in a long time.

I search for my keys as I turn the corner of my university building and when I look up, my heart freezes.

Emily stands in front of the door, her head turned skyward.

I stop abruptly, unsure of what to do. I examine her for a moment and remember the positive feeling I had after practice. Taking a deep breath, I straighten my shoulders and approach.

It's time to face her too.

16

Emily

After being firmly asked to leave the rink by Chase, I walked around campus for a while. Finally, my footsteps have brought me here, and I've been waiting for half an hour outside the door of Liam's residence. It takes all my courage to stand there and face him. But now that he's in front of me, I'm feeling increasingly nervous.

When he sees me, he stops for a moment, surprised. His gaze meets mine, and you can see the uncertainty in his eyes. A moment passes before he closes the distance between us. I take a deep breath. But I feel an invisible barrier between us, and my words tumble around in my mouth.

"Liam," I begin hesitantly. "I can explain everything..."

He looks at me and I can see an inner struggle raging inside him. It's as if he's torn between wanting to listen to me and being angry about the article.

Finally, he shakes his head.

"This time, I'm the one who needs time, Emily. I need to focus on my training and the game ahead."

My heart sinks at his words and I fight back tears. I was hoping he'd give me a chance to tell him I never meant to hurt him.

"I just want you to understand what really happened." I beg.

I'm ashamed of myself for begging for the attention I didn't want to give him after my altercation with his ex. He wanted to explain himself too, and I wouldn't listen. So, I'm getting my money's worth!

He shakes his head again and takes a step back, as if to protect himself from me, and I swallow my disappointment.

"Okay," I murmur. "When you're ready, let me know."

He nods weakly, opens the door, and disappears from my sight.

I'm left alone outside, and the feeling of helplessness overwhelms me. I'd really hoped to be able to resolve this quid pro quo tonight, but instead the gulf between us seems to have widened even further.

It's with a heavy heart that I head for my room.

★★★

Over the next few days, I spend a lot of time sorting out my thoughts and thinking about how we got here.

David, the editor-in-chief of the campus newspaper, flouted his authority, and my integrity for that matter, by carelessly altering the article about Liam. He had the nerve to sign my name to that piece of garbage! I'm extremely angry with him, but for the time being, I know he's untouchable. If I go after the editor, I'm going to get shot at point-blank range, because that guy's got connections. And he got his way by laughing in my face!

And what do I look like? Like the girl who knocked down her boyfriend to get some buzz...

I'm stuck between a feeling of shame and helplessness that knocks me out. I can barely concentrate on my classes. Cassy and Maddie can't get me out anywhere. I feel like I'm being stared at and made to look like a horrible person, so I prefer to keep to myself.

It's hard. Very hard.

Finally, I decide that I can't just sit back and do nothing. Liam and I have a history. Our feelings can't just be swept away overnight. Even if I was profoundly stupid to believe, even a little, in the words uttered by the infamous Sara. In fact, it wasn't that I believed her, it was that she hurt me by implying that what Liam did to me, he had done to others. For a moment, I was naive enough to believe that I was exceptional and that we were experiencing all our first times together. But I wasn't a virgin before I met him, and I've had one night stands and relationships too. But... I think I wanted to believe that we were experiencing something new together. Being reminded that it wasn't true hurt.

Poor idiot...

All of a sudden, my ego got the better of me and I braced myself. Now I'm paying the consequences.

So, I take my courage in both hands and decide to go to the last hockey game of the season, which takes place today with his team. It's crucial to his and Chase's future. If they place and win, they'll have a real shot at the draft! There's no way I'm going to miss it! Especially as scouts from all over the country will also be present, and this is their chance to shine after their intensive training over the past few weeks.

This time, no notebook or camera, no, it's okay, I gave it away! Another journalist from the campus newspaper was put on the case, and I'm relieved.

I find a place anonymously in the bleachers, a cap screwed on my head. I look really stupid, but I'd rather go incognito than get kicked out again or feel the stares of the other students weighing on me. Worse, to distract Liam from that fateful moment.

All around me, the atmosphere is electric. Die-hard fans are excited and hopeful.

For Liam and Chase, there's a lot more at stake than just winning or losing. They must be very nervous...

Thankfully, the article doesn't seem to have put a dent in Liam's training, and I commend his fortitude for that!

From the referee's first whistle, the fight is fierce. Their opponents are strong, and it seems they never miss an opportunity to provoke them. But neither Liam nor Chase is intimidated. They fight hard and show why they should play in the NHL.

Every shot, every save, every action on the ice has the potential to decide their future.

Towards the last few minutes of the game, with the score already well in favor of our university team, Liam starts to move. It's as if he's decided not to give up. He steals the puck and escapes with Chase towards the goal. It's a breathtaking moment and the spectators hold their breath. Liam passes to Chase at the last moment. He prepares himself, shoots, and puts the puck into the goal with force.

Shouts are heard everywhere, and I can't help but join in the fun.

They've won the season! It's unbelievable!

Already, many people are rushing to greet their victory. Coach Franklyn is thrilled, I can also see Mr. Turner, and several other journalists. It's great media coverage for them!

Without further ado, I descend a few levels towards the rink, waiting for the euphoria to die down a little before catching a glimpse of my favorite player.

After a moment, Liam sees me. An expression of surprise crosses his face, followed by a shy smile that warms my heart. I return it, and he finally winks at me. This simple little sign transports me, and I feel my whole body quake.

Does that mean he's no longer angry with me? Or is it the euphoria of the moment that makes him act this way?

But before I can get any closer, he's back with his teammates and disappears from my sight for a moment.

I'm about to turn back and head home, telling myself that he deserves to celebrate with dignity without me annoying him for the umpteenth time, when I hear my name behind me.

That voice I'd recognize in a thousand...

"Leaving already?"

I turn around and see him, his brown curls falling over his handsome face. He's absolutely gorgeous... Leaning against the edge of the rink, he's managed to escape for a moment, and I realize he's done it for me, when it's *his* moment.

"I... I didn't want to disturb you... And... congratulations! It was an exceptional game!"

He smiles broadly.

"Would you like to celebrate with me?"

I look at him hesitantly, not knowing on which foot to dance.

"Without you, it doesn't really make sense, to tell you the truth..." he adds, completing my decision to say yes.

"All right!"

I feel my heart skip a beat, but for all that, I mustn't think he's forgiven me everything. We must have a conversation, and I intend to do just that before the night is out.

"I'll text you the address of the party. See you there!"

He waves me off and goes back to his team. As for me, I hurry back inside to put on a suitable outfit and get rid of this damn cap.

Once there, I am surprised by the number of people present. The fraternity house that organized the event has not skimped on the alcohol and the atmosphere. It's almost as if they were sure our team would succeed!

Dressed in a short skirt, knee-high boots and a close-fitting top, I hope deep down I'm sexy enough to catch Liam's eye. There are a lot of people, and I suspect he'll be very busy. Never mind, I'll go for it, putting my feminist principles aside for the evening.

When I catch sight of him, I notice how relieved he seems that the pressure of the games is over. He's enjoying it, and I'm happy to see him like this. At least he's over that awful article and isn't hiding...

It's hard to get close to him, but eventually he sees me and comes to meet me.

"I'm glad you're here," he says, almost embarrassed.

We stare at each other for a moment before he opens his mouth to speak again, but the music is loud, and I can barely make out what he's saying.

"What?" I shout above the noise.

"I was saying I've been thinking and..."

Suddenly, a hand comes down on his shoulder, interrupting us. It's one of his teammates who brings him a beer and starts replaying the game with him.

It's going to be harder than I thought...

The hours fly by, and we haven't really had time to chat. The truth is, it's not the right time. I have to make up my mind. Just as I'm about to leave, I sense a presence at my back. I turn and face it, my knees suddenly soft.

"Can I walk home with you?" asks Liam.

The question surprises me, but I can see the nostalgia in his eyes. I nod without a word, far too stressed for what's to come.

On the way home, we're pretty quiet. As he doesn't seem to want to leave me on my doorstep, full of apprehension, I let him in. Fortunately, Cassy is away with her family for a few days. So, we have the room to ourselves.

When the door closes, the atmosphere becomes a little more tense.

"Liam..."

"No, wait a minute. I'd like to speak first."

I nod.

"I'm sorry my ex said all those horrible things at the Spring Gala. She was wrong about everything. Because with you, it's different. Very different. I'm not the guy she knew. And no, despite what you wrote, I wanted to tell you in person: I've never had anything to do with drugs. That was her problem, her addictions, and I left her partly because of that. And also because, at the time, I wasn't seriously considering a relationship.

I swallow, digesting all this information.

"I didn't write this article."

His eyes widen in surprise.

"I knew it!" he exclaims.

"But the look on your face makes me think I've just told you I'm the Queen of England."

"Rho, Em! It's not that! It's just that, deep down, I couldn't convince myself that you'd written that load of crap. It's a relief to know."

"How could you think for a moment that I could write that?"

I'm a little offended to hear it in person.

"Don't blame me! I mean when your girlfriend, with whom you've finally decided to have a serious relationship and whom you love, ends up with her name at the end of something despicable..."

It's my turn to round my mouth and widen my eyes.

"And you were so angry after the altercation with Sara, so disappointed..." he continues.

Seeing that I'm still not saying anything, he continues.

"What's up? Why the long face? This time, it looks like I'm the one who just told you I'm the Pope."

"No, but you just said you loved me..."

"Oh... I..."

I approach him to end the distance between us. My hands rest on his forearms, and I find his strength, and his warmth.

What I missed... More than I could admit to myself...

"Well, yes, I love you, Emily. It's out of control. Scary, too. But so good and amazing. You knock me down with a bat of the eye and pick me up with a smile. You consume me with a kiss, or with a particularly sexy evening gown..."

He smirks at the memory of our torrid embrace before the end-of-spring, Gala. I laugh softly.

"I love you, Liam. It's just as uncontrollable and unbelievable. And it scares me too. But what I do know, and at least what these last few days have proven to me, is that I can't imagine my life without you."

I feel his breath quicken against my mouth, and my heart starts to race.

"And the article, it was David the editor who took the liberty of taking it back from me before it was published. I hadn't written that at all! So yes, he had asked me to find some gossip, and I should have told you about it beforehand, but I thought I could avoid writing it and move on. Except he threatened to tell the *New York Post that* I was being picky and all..."

"What an asshole!"

"As a result, when I read what he'd published, I wanted to report him. Maddie talked me out of it, though she was as disgusted by his behavior as I was. The guy's got a stranglehold on the campus newspaper and a lot of connections. If I said anything, denial or otherwise, he'd blow me up with a snap of his fingers, and word would get out. Everything gets out in this business, not to mention the fact that the guy will do anything to protect himself by ruining others."

"I can understand that. Your career was also at stake…"

"I wanted to tell you, but…"

"But I wouldn't listen."

"You had to concentrate on your training, and you were right! It paid off. I'm so proud!"

He smiles, almost blushing.

"We chose our respective passions, at the risk of jeopardizing our love," he says.

"How about a promise that this will never happen again?"

He nods and leans toward me, his lips very close to mine.

"Emily, I swear I'll talk to you about everything from now on. And that nothing will ever stand in the way of our relationship again."

"Liam, I swear the same."

Finally, he kisses me and it's as if the ground opens up beneath my feet. He holds me tighter and grunts with pleasure as our tongues mingle. Stumbling backwards, we make our way to my bedroom, where we frantically strip off our clothes.

I need to feel him against me. His skin, his breath, his kisses…

Liam kisses me passionately and I feel myself getting hotter. I wrap my legs around him and let my hands roam up and down his back.

"I've missed you so much," he murmurs between kisses.

He places little kisses on every inch of my body.

When he reaches between my legs, I let out a little cry of pleasure. With his tongue and fingers, he slowly sweeps me off my feet. I think I'm about to explode when he jerks me around. He caresses my back and gently bites the back of my neck. His caresses are electrifying. I need more than this, I need him.

My hips develop a life of their own and tense towards him.

When he finally penetrates me, a great sigh escapes me. To be one with him is amazing. With steady strokes, he pushes me into ecstasy and just as I'm recovering from this wave of pleasure, he turns me over again and pulls me onto his lap. I lean down and kiss him, letting my mouth move from his lips to his neck and torso, while my hips slowly rotate. Liam's hands sink into my butt and he moans softly. Soon after, a new wave of pleasure washes over me and my legs tremble. Liam smiles in satisfaction and looks at me lovingly before turning me onto my back. After a few quick thrusts, he too falls off the cliff and collapses on top of me. We both breathe hard as our bodies recover.

Finally, Liam slides over and pulls me against him. He holds me tight, and we fall asleep. Together.

Rays of sunlight tickle my nose and I wake up gently. At the memory of our reunion, I smile like an idiot and stretch out, careful not to wake my beautiful sleeper.

I get up to prepare coffee and breakfast for us when the door suddenly opens.

Cassy stands in the doorway, wide-eyed at who she sees in my bed, and a big smile spreads across her face.

"Wild night?" she asks, laughing.

I blush immediately and step in front of her to block her view.

"I'm glad you were able to sort out your problems, sweetie," she continues, giving me a hug.

"Liam's still asleep, so please, could you..."

But already in my bed, the sheets are stirring.

"Oh, hi Cassy..."

"Hi Liam!"

She doesn't seem the least bit embarrassed. Finally, she turns away and finishes preparing the breakfast I've left unfinished. Liam takes the opportunity to put on his pants and T-shirt, before coming over to give me a delicate kiss.

"Hello," he says serenely, running a hand through his hair.

Cassy hides her smile behind her coffee cup, and I nudge her gently, which only makes her smile more.

We eat breakfast without speaking to each other, but a pleasant silence envelops the three of us.

Later, Liam and I go for a walk in the campus park. He tells me about his training sessions and how he's preparing for the draft. I admire his ambition and am determined to support him in this. We also talk about my career as a journalist and how we can better reconcile our passions and our relationship.

"Have you ever thought of specializing in sports reporting, Em?"

"Uh... Not really, no..."

But that doesn't mean it's a stupid idea.

"You're really good at conveying the atmosphere of a game, and you know a lot about it now, at least about hockey."

"That's right, it could be a good idea!"

"And it would save you from having to write articles on juicy subjects, which doesn't seem to be your forte."

He laughs at that last sentence, and I blush.

"Yes, it would be a thorn in my side! I hate that kind of journalism... You're right, I'll think about it!"

He smiles at me, and gently takes my hand before placing a kiss on it.

Scandalous journalism has never been my cup of tea, and perhaps a specialization would clarify my path a little more.

When we arrive back at my place, we both feel like we're starting a new chapter. It's not perfect, but we're ready to work on strengthening our relationship and overcoming obstacles together.

I'm determined to make a change professionally too. I've already gained experience in sports reporting and it's time for me to forge my own path.

17

Emily

Not surprisingly, my decision to focus on sports reporting brings with it new professional challenges. My supervisor at the *New York Post* has accepted my proposal, but I still have to prove myself. Interns don't have the freedom to choose what they want to do, and I had to explain my plans and motivations in great detail to change his mind. Now it's up to me to prove to him that he was right to put his trust in me.

The first few weeks were not easy. I've been greeted with skeptical looks and mistrust within the sports editorial team. But I don't let that discourage me, and I work hard to make a place for myself. With time, some people begin to recognize my skills and I gradually earn their respect.

Meanwhile, I continue to support Liam in his hockey career. He continues to train and I'm proud of his commitment.

Our relationship is evolving and we're managing to keep a strong bond, even if the time we spend together is limited. *Facetime*, a little coffee date, love letters under doors - we're on the right track.

I'm typing frantically on my laptop when my supervisor, Mr. Roberts, approaches me at a brisk pace.

"Emily, I need you today at Madison Square Garden. The reporter who was supposed to follow the game is sick and you'll have to replace him," he says hastily.

My pulse quickens instantly.

"The New York Rangers game? You want me to cover that?" I ask, incredulous.

He nods.

"You know a lot about ice hockey, and we don't have any other replacements on hand who we could train. Hurry up, the game starts in two hours!"

Adrenalin rushes through my veins and I nod eagerly.

"I'll get started right away!"

It's a huge opportunity for me.

Hands trembling, I pack up my press card, laptop and recorder. I'll do my best to provide a good report!

I'm happy to rush off, ready to take on my first assignment as a sports journalist for such an important game.

My belly quivers with excitement.

The Rangers are the team Liam would dream of joining and, thanks to the work of Mr. Turner, the agent who works with him and Chase, the NHL seems within reach for them.

I can't believe it! Not only am I accompanying Liam on his journey, but I'm also taking big steps towards my dream career.

The tension in the air is palpable as I enter the huge arena. Excited fans, dressed in Rangers jerseys and scarves, sing in unison in support of the team.

When I take my place, I'm very nervous. It's the first time I've sat in an official press box, surrounded by other journalists. The atmosphere is absolutely indescribable. I can't believe I'm here with all these famous sports journalists. I sneak a *selfie* and send it to the girls and Liam. This moment has to be immortalized!

Icebound Attraction

The arena is abuzz as the two teams take to the ice. The line-up is announced and the first whistle blows.
The game begins.
The Rangers enter the match strongly and immediately exert pressure on their opponents' goal. It's a very tight game and their opponents are not easily intimidated.

Midway through the first period, the Rangers' defender manages to retrieve the puck and make a precise pass to his attacking partner, who score the game's first goal. The arena literally explodes with joy.

The game goes back and forth, with chances on both sides, and the tension mounts as we enter the final minutes, and the Rangers lead by a narrow margin. Finally, when the final siren sounds, the Rangers have won!

I jump out of my seat and exult loudly. The other journalists look at me quizzically. As a journalist, I'm supposed to be impartial...

I can hardly contain my enthusiasm as I take my notes for the report. This game had everything an ice hockey fan could want: suspense, drama and passion. It's a whole new level of hockey compared to university games, let's face it!

I hope I'll be able to convey everything I feel and deliver an exciting article.

Emily, let's get to work!

★★★

Heart pounding, I move back and forth in my seat. The big day has finally arrived!

Today is the annual NHL draft, and we are in Nashville for the occasion. Bridgestone Arena is impressive in its size and packed with an incredible crowd. Several TV crews are also on hand to broadcast the event on the sports channels, and

I'm craning my neck to catch a glimpse of a few journalists I really like.

Liam fidgets nervously beside me. He's wearing a blue suit, a white shirt and a matching blue tie that sets off his bright eyes.

I place my hand gently on his and smile.

"It's going to be all right, my love."

He smiles gratefully, but his tension doesn't disappear.

I let my gaze wander around the room. Many NHL prospects fill this section of the arena, most accompanied by their families.

I sigh inwardly. Liam's family unfortunately couldn't make the trip to support him. But Chase and I are at his side.

The latter seems no less feverish than his best friend. The two regularly give each other feverish glances.

At this point, the evening's host gets on the stage, and the conversation stops.

"Ladies and gentlemen, welcome to the sixty-first draft in NHL history! I'm glad you're all here to share in the excitement of our young talent and our teams. The draft is something very special. It's the beginning of a future that can change lives."

Significantly, he lets his gaze sweep over the arena and a shiver runs through my body. So many people have worked hard for this big day!

"I invite the Chicago Blackhawks to take the microphone!" he announces.

A muscular man in a black suit enters the stage and clears his throat. He makes a brief speech, thanks the team and sponsors, then looks out at the crowd for a few seconds. A mischievous smile appears on his face.

"I'm sure you'd all like to know our team's choice for this first round. I'm sorry to keep you waiting, but it's always a pleasure to do so."

Icebound Attraction

The room erupts in collective laughter.

"The Chicago Blackhawks elect Chase Carter this year!"

Chase jumps to his feet, mouth open. He runs his hands through his hair.

"Dude! Congratulations!" exclaims Liam, tapping him on the shoulder.

They give each other a quick hug and Chase makes his way to the stage. After a few emotional words of thanks, he puts on his shirt and looks in our direction.

"Liam, my brother, without you, I wouldn't be here. Thank you for everything!"

Liam's eyes shine with restrained emotion and he applauds his best friend loudly.

I'm also very happy for him. The Chicago Blackhawks were high on his list. He was selected first and has now passed the stress test!

Liam smiles as he sits back down, but his excitement is palpable. I stroke his hand gently.

Round after round, players are drafted one after the other by the teams. Already, the first exchanges are taking place, and the number of places is dwindling. The tension mounts a little more each time, and Liam's name has yet to be called.

My heart skips a beat when the New York Rangers' goalkeeper steps up to the microphone. Excited, I rub my hands together and cast a sidelong glance at Liam. He looks petrified.

The broad-shouldered man's voice echoes through the loudspeakers.

"Good evening, ladies and gentlemen. I'll be brief for this penultimate round, as I know some of you are anxiously awaiting our pick. The New York Rangers would like to draft... Adam Peterson."

The room is going wild, but something inside me is crumbling. Liam still hasn't moved, but I can clearly feel his disappointment in my heart. The choices are starting to narrow, and there aren't many seats left...

"Since we traded one of our draft picks in the previous round, we still have a choice for this one. One we'd love to have on our team," says the goalie's husky voice. Liam squeezes my hand so hard it feels like it's going to break.

"Liam Scott, how would you like to join the Rangers?"

Liam's gaze turns to me. Tears of joy glisten in his eyes.

"Oh... My love... I did it. I really did it!"

Excited, I take his hand and look deeply into his eyes.

We stand up together and I pull him against me.

At that moment, it's as if time no longer exists. Surrounded by applause, we are in each other's arms. We've both hoped so hard for this outcome, and yet I can't believe it. Liam is going to play for the New York Rangers and start a whole new chapter in his life. I couldn't be prouder of him.

He takes the stage, beaming, A Rangers jersey in hand.

"Wow... I am incredibly grateful for this opportunity, and I would like to thank a very special person. Emily, I love you! And Chase, I'm already looking forward to our first game!"

He smiles to thunderous applause.

Pride and love flood my heart. This is the beginning of something very big for us and I couldn't be happier.

EPILOGUE

Liam

Three years later

I could only imagine the changes that a contract with the Rangers would entail, but now that I look at the stunning apartment in the heart of the Upper East Side where I live with Emily, I'm amazed. It's been a long road, a lot of hard work and concessions for beautiful results, which now allow us to have a home together.

The city that never sleeps seems perfectly suited to our relationship - vibrant, lively and exciting.

My hockey career also continues to flourish. I'm still playing for the New York Rangers and have become quite well known in the league. The experience I've gained on the ice is priceless, and I'm happy to be living my dream.

Emily is in the final stages of her studies and progressing in her career as a sports journalist. Her articles are being read by more and more people, and she's starting to make a name for herself in the industry. I admire her ambition and am proud to be at her side.

I look out of the large bay window overlooking the city. As Christmas approaches, the streets of New York are decked out in festive decorations, and there's a very special atmosphere.

We decided to invite our family and friends to celebrate the festive season together, and they all turned up.

The large dining table in our apartment overflows with dishes, each more appetizing than the last, while laughter and conversation fill the room.

"Liam, you played so well in your last game!" exclaims my mother proudly.

Once she saw that I could make a good living from hockey and that I was fully happy, she changed her mind about my career. Today, she supports me as much as she can. This has given our relationship the stable foundation it lacked before, and I'm grateful that we've reached this point.

Chase and Cassy are talking animatedly to Emily's mother, while her father sits stoically beside them. I smile. He really is one of a kind. Although he rarely expresses his feelings, his love for his family is palpable at every turn. As for Maddie, she seems to be debating a fascinating subject with Coach Franklyn and Mr. Turner.

After I was drafted, I made a point of keeping in touch with them. They were the driving forces behind my success. I'll always be eternally grateful to them.

In a corner of the living room, I spot my sisters and Emily's sisters laughing. It sometimes hurts that I'm the only man around when they get together, but hey, as long as they're happy, I'm happy too! To our delight, the four of them get on wonderfully well together.

I tighten my grip on Emily's hand and watch my beautiful blonde. I can feel how much we've grown; how much we're loved and supported. Our love for each other has also grown stronger with each passing year. We have an exciting and fulfilling future ahead of us. Together, we've overcome obstacles, fulfilled dreams and strengthened our relationship.

As our guests make their way home and the door closes behind Emily's father, she wraps her arms around my neck.

"What do you say we start our own Christmas tradition? A vacation together, or something like that?" she asks.

I smile at the thought.

"That's a good idea, my love! Do you have anything special in mind?"

We sit comfortably on the sofa and exchange ideas.

Finally, we have the idea of a road trip to Vermont. The idea of snow-covered landscapes, a cozy cottage and a romantic atmosphere for a few days immediately captivates us both. Sitting in front of a fireplace with Emily, while it's snowing outside... I can't imagine anything more beautiful.

We immediately set about looking for a place. We search the offers and opt for a charming hotel on the edge of a small mountain village. It promises to be warm and welcoming, with breathtaking views, and the perfect place to spend the rest of our vacation.

Emily looks at me with a mischievous smile.

"What if we leave now, right away, without thinking too much?"

I raise my eyebrows and stand speechless for a moment. But why not? We have no obligations at the moment and can devote ourselves entirely to each other.

In response, I simply pull her against me and kiss her passionately. I love her spontaneity. Every day with her is an adventure and I'm so incredibly happy that we've overcome all the obstacles of the past.

After throwing a few clothes into a suitcase, we settle into the car and drive off, slowly leaving the city behind.

The roads are covered with a thick layer of snow, and the winter landscape around us is breathtaking. More than once,

Icebound Attraction

I look at Emily out of the corner of my eye and the corners of my mouth automatically turn up.

We arrive at the hotel in the early hours of the morning. Our room is adorned with Christmas decorations and a fire is already crackling in the fireplace, bringing warmth and comfort.

Emily beams with joy.

"Magnificent!"

Seeing her like this warms my heart.

We immediately explore the surrounding area, passing through picturesque villages, visiting a Christmas market and sampling regional specialties. We stroll through snow-covered landscapes and enjoy the silence that this season brings. It's as if we can deepen our love on a whole new level here.

We spend Christmas Eve in front of the fireplace, exchanging gifts. And while she gazes dreamily at the new camera in her hands, I rummage in my pocket.

My heart beats wildly as I clear my throat and Emily looks at me quizzically.

"I know you don't think much of gifts, but I've got something for you…" I declare.

She frowns.

"Don't keep me in suspense! Give it to me!" she jokes, giggling.

I smile nervously and search for the right words.

"Okay, so… Shit… It always looks so easy in the movies."

Emily's mouth rounds and she looks at me in disbelief. Just then, I open the box containing a ring that I'm holding in my hands.

"My love, you're the woman I've always dreamed of. I love you more than anything, and I want to show it to you every day. Emily Hansen, will you be my happiness? Say yes to us, forever?"

I now have tears in my eyes and can't see straight. I run my hand over my face nervously and look at Emily expectantly. She seems to be in a state of shock.

"Earth to Emily! An answer would be pretty good for my nerves."

She snaps out of her torpor and climbs onto my lap.

"Of course I do, Liam! Forever - just you and me!"

I slide the ring onto her finger and smile. Her lips rest gently on mine for a long kiss.

For a moment, I break our embrace to seek out her gaze. This is a very special moment, and I want to remember the expression in her eyes forever. Those eyes, which have enchanted me thousands of times before, now carry a special glow.

I find her mouth again and we kiss passionately before I lay Emily down on the rug in front of the fireplace.

"Words don't do this feeling justice, but... I love you, Liam. I love you so much!"

"I love you too, my future wife," I reply, and we smile lovingly at each other.

It promises to be a delicious evening.

Our books are also available in e-book. Find our catalog on:
https://cherry-publishing.com/en/

Subscribe to our newsletter and receive a free e-book! You'll also receive the latest updates on all of our upcoming publications!

https://mailchi.mp/b78947827e5e/get-your-free-ebook

Editorial manager: Audrey Puech
Composition and layout: Cherry Publishing
Interior Illustrations: © Shutterstock
Cover design: Keti Matakov
Cover illustration: Keti Matakov

Made in the USA
Columbia, SC
21 June 2025